FOR LIN CASCIATO

PRAISE FOR *THE SKY BETWEEN YOU AND ME*

"Sit quietly with this book. Feel the wind, the dusty air. Taste the sorrow and the wonder. Listen to the heart that is beating on every page. Then be grateful that Catherine Alene gave us this stunning story. It's a thing of beauty."

—Kathi Appelt, Newbery Honor and
National Book Award finalist

"A breathtaking and unforgettable debut. Alene weaves verse as carefully as Raesha runs a barrel racer course—with precision and grace, and her tale of anorexia is authentic and heart-wrenching. This is a layered tale of romance, loss, and friendship that can't be missed. I can't wait for Alene's next work."

—Jessica Burkhart, author of the Canterwood
Crest series and *Wild Hearts*

"In evocative verse, author Catherine Alene whittles Raesha's world down to bone, as her need to be thin carves away her flesh, friends, and family. Honest, unflinching, and painfully beautiful, *The Sky between You and Me* is a gift of understanding and hope to those who struggle and the ones who love them."

—Catherine Linka, author of *A Girl Called Fearless*

"Alene doesn't sensationalize eating disorders, rather authentically portrays the internal struggle they pose while respectfully refraining from assigning numbers (pounds, inches, calories, grams, clothing sizes, time) that may be triggering for suffering and recovering readers alike. And she does it with a narrative style that is not only highly engaging, but lyrical. This combination makes an intensely haunting story also a beautiful one."

—Sarah Alexander, licensed clinical social worker

"Alene, a recovering anorexic, skillfully conveys Raesha's increasing withdrawal from worried friends and her fixation on counting calories and exercising. But this is much more than a problem novel. Raesha's Western world is beautifully evoked, from the 'breathed blue' of the sky to the camaraderie between the girl and her horse and dog."

—*The Washington Post*

"This powerful tale is a realistic portrayal of the difficulties many go through every day with an eating disorder."

—PopCrush.com

"This debut provides and intriguing and valuable perspective."

—*Booklist*

"Raw and heartbreaking. Alene's work tackles a very sensitive topic with accuracy and compassion. This title will resonate with readers on many levels."

—*School Library Journal*

THE
SKY
BETWEEN
YOU
and
ME

CATHERINE ALENE

sourcebooks
fire

Published by Sourcebooks Fire, an imprint of Sourcebooks, Inc.
P.O. Box 4410, Naperville, Illinois 60567-4410
(630) 961-3900
Fax: (630) 961-2168
www.sourcebooks.com

Library of Congress Cataloging-in-Publication data is on file with the publisher.

Printed and bound in the United States of America.
VP 10 9 8 7 6 5 4 3 2 1

ROUNDUP

We started this morning
Before the sun leaked across the sky
While the steers were stiff and slow with cold

It was as it has always been
Men and women and kids
Slumped against pickup trucks
Inhaling the steam off their coffee
All in chinks and boots with jingling spurs
Horses tacked up
Lead ropes looped through the slats of stock trailers
And the dogs zipping in and out of it all
Heeler dogs
Cow-eating machines

Asia and me
Best friends since forever
First to be mounted up and ready to go
Same as we have since we were three
Old enough to ride
Old enough to work

Sixteen now
Still riding
Still working
Asia with her white-blond hair and Scuba, her palomino paint
Her little sister, Alexi, on her horse named Putty right behind

1

Me and Asia are whoopin'
At the cattle to get it all started
When Dad lopes up on his fancy new bay and joins in
Lanky arms waving
Hand slapping his leg

Horses stomp themselves awake as riders swing into the saddle
Neighbors, parents, brothers, sisters, aunts, uncles, cousins
It's all the same today
When even a family
That's only a pair
Like me and Dad
Suddenly have more family than we can count

SAGEBRUSH AFTERNOON

Rawhide daydreams
    Spun
    Beneath a sky burned
       White

Trailing cows
    Between
       Snarls of sage

Fastest way to move cows is at a walk
So we do
Fanning out around
       behind
     beside
The cattle coming in to be
Doctored

Dad's voice pulls me out of my daydream
Back to the cows
"Ride ahead and make sure the gates are set."
Asia's dad flicks Scuba's hindquarters with the tip of his reins and
Laughs as Scuba pricks his ears
"Help her, Asia."

That's when I see
The two-tone horse trailer
Hitched to the rusted-out
Dented-in

Orange truck
Pulling up to the barn

I know it's bad
Terrible actually
To let your horse run back to the barn
But I can't help it

I lie
Against Fancy's neck
Clamp my hat to my head with my hand
Lean into the wind we're creating

Cody and Micah see us coming
Pull their horses' heads out of the grass
Catch their stirrups with their left legs
Swing up and on
Their horses already running
Into a game of chicken
We never let
Go wrong
Micah at Asia
Cody at me
Knowing the horses will swerve

Fancy's already pulling to the left
Her strong lead
As Cody bears down
Riding the thunder rolling
Under his horse's hooves

My eyes fill with dust so sharp
I'm blinking across sandpaper at Cody
His horse the color of a chocolate bar
Wearing marshmallow socks
Swerving to his left
I to mine
Corkscrewing around
Toward each other

We lean out of our laughter
And into each other
For a kiss shared behind the cloud of dust
Kicked up by the cattle coming our way

And we're off again
Leaning into the same wind this time
As we ride to the herd
Where Asia and Micah are already slapping their ropes
Shimmied round
Against their legs
Limbering up for the roping
That comes with the sorting
Just before the chute

BONE-TIRED

Dust starched jeans in a crumpled heap
Blue turns around
    once
        twice
    three times
        and calls them his bed

Wind-singed cheeks
Eyes blown red
I surrender
Tired limbs luxuriating in the embrace of flannel sheets

My stomach snarls
Angry
Empty

Breakfast
Coffee
Black
No time for much else

Lunch
Chased a calf down from the mesa
No time for much else

Dinner
Cody and Micah in their orange Ford
Come to help in a spray of gravel
I was so busy talking to Cody

Fireflies in my chest
No time for much else

Palm
Pressed flat
To my stomach

And the hunger
Is gone

IT SEEMS

It's the dust and the noise
Cattle bawling
Squeeze chute clanging
Dogs barking
Snapping at the air
As they heel right
Push left

Neighbors, parents, brothers, sisters, aunts, uncles, cousins
All working hard again
Same as they did yesterday
Sorting the cattle we brought in
For the ear tagging and doctoring that will come today

I know them all
Close as family
Except this new girl
With gold hair chasing down her back
Riding up to the pens
Coming in through the gate

I would have noticed
That girl
Any girl
On a buckskin gelding as fancy as that
Working with us
Especially since she wasn't here yesterday
Showed up this morning
Midway through roundup

But she's doing fine
Moving fast
Someone's cousin maybe
No time to wonder
In the middle of all this work
That needs doing

Asia and I ride through the crush of
    skunk-backed
        bald-faced
            solid-blacks
Pushing and bawling
In and out and through the pens

Even my dog's working
Fills me up
Makes me proud
To watch Blue run the cattle
Runs them tight to the chute
Then ducks under the fence
Races around to pick up more

Races right behind that girl
That girl on the buckskin horse
That buckskin horse whose hind hoof comes flying
Sends Blue flying
Hitting the dirt with blood running into his eyes

I'm off my horse
Slapping at the cattle to get past
Screaming

At those cows
Trampling him

Knowing that I can't do life
Without him
Not without Blue

MY DOG

Blue
Pulling himself under the fence
Crying
        Crying
I catch him up
Hold him close

Blue's eyes are all wrong
One pupil bigger than the other
Blood rolling
From the half-moon kick
Just below his ear

Dad saw it too
Is here now
Running his hands over Blue's sides
Cody passes him a bandanna through the fence
Dad presses it against Blue's head
Then we're all in the truck
Cody's talking into his cell
Calling ahead to let Dr. Katy know we're coming

Blue
His head pressed into my lap
Shaking with pain that shivers along his sides
Absorbs through my legs
Fills up my chest
Makes it hard to breathe
To hear Dad's voice

Over the sound of my heart breaking
Hearing only my dog, my dog, my dog crying

Ragged tears fall
From my eyes that can't see
So full of saline and fear
But know we are here
Spraying gravel 'round the drive
At the part-house, part-clinic
Dr. Katy's resting place healing space
Where she takes Blue from my arms
It'll be okay, she says with her eyes
His wound
My heart

Dad's hand on my shoulder guides me through the living room
Down the hall
Into the room smelling of Betadine and gauze
Holds me strong
Alongside the exam table where she lays Blue
My heart
So broken and small beneath her plastic-gloved hands

Dr. Katy pulls the bandanna off Blue's forehead
Stiff with blood dried black
Cold hot cold behind my eyes
My legs are liquid
One hand on Blue's shoulder
The other curled around the edge of the table
Squeezing the metal
      So tight my knuckles go white
      So tight it hurts

So tight that I almost don't have to think
About the fact that this is what I do
Break everything I love
Then cry when it's gone

This is
My fault
I should have watched him closer
Especially around a new horse
Because I know horses
I know dogs, and I should have seen it coming
I shouldn't have let it happen

Blue's panting like he's run miles
Staring straight into me
Dr. Katy pushes the needle into his hip
Blue whimpers
I wish it would work now
Now
The drugs can't relax his pain fast enough in this minute that
    seems like forever
Blue's eyes droop shut
Slowly
Slowly

"He'll be okay."
Dad says it first
A statement
Not a question
"He will." Dr. Katy's eyes only see Blue as she cleans his
    wound
Wipes the blood

AFTER THE FACT

"I bet he won't even have a scar," Dr. Katy says.
I take the amber-colored bottles
That rattle with pills
From her hands
The same kind of bottles
That stood along the windowsill
    in my parents' bathroom
In a line that grew longer and longer
As Mom got sicker and sicker

I haven't thought about that in forever
The way the sun made the plastic glow
When it hit the bottles just right
Arranged from tallest to shortest
Label side out

That was then
This is now
I know that
But I want to throw the bottles against the wall
I tuck them into the pocket of my coat instead

Cody catches the door
Dad lifts Blue off the table
I'm at his elbow
Keeping my hand on Blue's hip
Dr. Katy walks us out to the truck, where I climb in first
Cody right behind

Dad lays Blue across my lap
Quiet now
His weight, his warmth, feels good against my legs
I press my hand against his ribs just behind his front leg
His heart against my palm

Dad climbs in
Starts the truck
Tosses a wave through the rear window at Dr. Katy
Standing in the drive watching us pull away
"She's an awful sweet lady, isn't she? One hell of a vet."

She is.
My fingers find the bottles in my pocket
Does Dad remember?
That row of amber plastic?
Was he the one who threw them away after she was gone?

The question
Doesn't clear my mind
Just settles my thoughts
Enough for her to slip in

The fields running past
My dog in my lap
I didn't think about how
She slid off her buckskin horse
Hands over her mouth
Tear-clotted words slipping between her fingers
"I'm sorry—
    I'm so sorry—"

That's all she kept saying
Whoever she was

TRADITION

"Get out of here," Dad says
Following my eyes to the couch
Where Blue snores
"I've got this. He'll be fine."

So Cody and I tack up our horses and ride
This Sunday
Like every Sunday
Since seventh grade
Hooves clip-clopping
Up Main Street
    What else would the only street with a stoplight be called
      but Main

Destination—
Tracy's Diner
Where the only seating available is either
    in your rig
        on your saddle
            or at one of the picnic tables
Slouched in the grassy patch off to the side of the restaurant
Where me, Cody, and everyone else in this alfalfa-sweet town
Has carved their brand into the benches worn slick

The drive-in, ride-through diner
Tracy sold off
To Dale and his wife Tawny
Seven years ago
They even changed the name on the sign from

Tracy's
To Tawny and Dale's
But Tracy owned it first, so her name's still stuck to it
Tight as tradition

We climb off our horses
Pull off their bridles
Hang them from the hitching post
Leaving the horses free to wander
To get down to the business of grazing
Hay burners that they are

Tawny, with her hair teased up stiff as porcupine quills,
Greets us at the window
Asks, "How you two been?"
Handing curly fries
Seasoned of course
Cokes and ice cream cones
Through the window without us even ordering
Pausing as she reaches under the counter
Where the dog biscuits are stored
"Where's Blue?" she asks.
And I explain
About the stitches and him resting now
He'll be okay
She nods
Give me the dog biscuits to go

We set the fries and Cokes on the picnic table
And call our horses to us
Fancy trots over
Her nostrils flaring

Lips quivering
Already tasting the vanilla soft-serve sliding down her throat
She licks her cone
Sending rivulets of melted ice cream streaming down my hand

Cody's gelding chomps into his
Ice cream in one bite
Cone in the second
Quick as that and back to grazing

Cody knows without asking
We'll be heading back earlier than we usually do
But we enjoy it just the same
Chipping away with our straws at the ice in our Cokes
Cody swirling fry after fry across the sauce
Mayonnaise and ketchup stirred pink
Nodding in agreement at all the right times
As we
Mostly I
Talk about everything
Laughing at nothing

Because that's how we do it
Boyfriend and girlfriend
But most of all
Friends

FUGUE

Blue and I are shadows
Curled together on the living room floor
Just the two of us
Now that Dad has gone to bed

Blue kicks
A snuffle snore wrinkles his nose
He's dreaming
Something that I wish I could do
On nights like this when I know
Sleep
Won't come

I slide out from under the weight
Of the night
Running my index finger gently
Over the staples and stitches
Criss-crossing Blue's head
Before I slip
Into the kitchen

I turn on the light
Above the stove
To find the clear custard bowl
In the cupboard
Between the stacks of plates and mugs

To fish out the silver teaspoon
Etched with roses

That lives in the back of the silverware drawer
Too small for me to use
During the day

The only spoon I'll use for this
Nighttime ritual
Certain to soothe
When my mind won't stop
    run
        run
            running
Over what
    could have
        should have
            would have
If only I had, hadn't, would have, could have done
What?

I open the cupboard
Above the stove
And reach behind the canister of flour
For the yellow bag
That crinkles beneath my fingertips

Splenda
The zero-calorie sweetener
We keep on hand
For guests
At least that's what Dad thinks
Not knowing that I empty
And replace
The bag myself

Because I go through a lot
On nights like this
When I fill the custard bowl
Nearly to the top

Silver spoon in my right hand
Salt shaker in my left
Dip and pour
A spoonful of Splenda
Covered in salt
Laid on my tongue
Where it burns

Spoon after spoon
It calms my mind
Until the Splenda
Is gone

PERFECT REMEDY

I'd been shameless this morning
Stretched out on the couch
With Blue draped across my lap
Come on, Dad. Let us come! I can't leave Blue.

Standing there in the kitchen with his boots in his hand
Dad had tried to look stern
"Just this once," he'd said.
But he'd put me to work
Would need help loading cattle
High-headed, wild things from a ranch northwest of here
Couldn't do it alone

I used to beg to go with him
When I was little
Rode shotgun in the cab
Through states the colors of sunflowers and clay to load them
Bulls, calves, cows pressed together tight
Bawling and swaying with the rhythm of the road

We're off the couch and out the front door
Before he can change his mind
The truck is unlocked
Diesel engine rumbling
Warming up
For the trek

I heft Blue in
Crawl into the back

Settle him on the bed behind the seats
Cozy on the horse print blanket
Worn fuzzy by my childhood hands
When the headlights came on
Hugged into sleep by Dad's voice
Humming quiet behind the radio

It's been a long time
Since I've ridden like this
With Dad
But his truck is the same
Only with more wallet-sized mes
One for each year
Taped in rows across Dad's sun visor
Always down

Blue wags his stumpy tail as Dad climbs in
"Ready, hookies?" he asks.

The truck groans forward
Dad leans down
Eyes on the road
Grabs a box of Captain Crunch mashed half-flat
From under his seat
Gives it to me and puts out his hand
Some for him
Some for Blue
Poured on the blanket in front of his nose

The smell of peanut butter
Fills the cab
I tuck the lid closed

Slide the box under my seat
Not hungry at all
Because all I need is this
My dad beside me
My dog behind me

We're a team
Of three

UNEXPECTED VISITOR

Twenty-four hours later
Blue's up
I'm down
Until he starts barking
Waking me from my nap on the couch

The doorbell rings
Which is redundant
Since Blue's dancing around the living room
Blue, settle.
It feels so good to say that
He drops to a sit
Stares at the door
Wills me to open it

Cody or Asia
Would have come in without ringing
I wasn't expecting her
That girl with the gold hair chasing down her back
Standing on our front porch
An African violet in one hand
A shrink-wrapped knucklebone in the other
The marinated kind they sell at the feed store

Which makes me think of Cody
How that's what he gave me
The first time we went out
Flowers for me
A bone for Blue

Because he knew me that well
Even then

"Hi. I'm Kierra. I hope it's okay I came by, but I had to tell you
    in person how sorry I am."
Pressure cooker sentences
Come out so fast they color her cheeks pink
She looks past me
Into the living room
Where Blue is still sitting
Front paws anchored
Hind end wiggling as fast as his tail would be waving
If it wasn't docked

"How is he?"
Better.
I fold my arms across my chest
Remembering the way the pain
Shivered
Up Blue's sides
As he lay across my lap
In the truck
"I brought this for him. For you. A get-well-soon gift."
She holds out the plant and bone

I hate myself
For letting the chasm appear between us
When her words stop
But I can't forgive and forget
Not with the echo
Of my dog, my dog, my dog crying
Still in my ears

Behind me Blue breaks
Explodes out of his sit
The bone
He can see it
Knows it's for him

The metal screen door is cool
Against my palm
As I push it open
Step back
Welcome her in

She's thin
Thinner than me
Maybe
Maybe not
Not that it matters
When you're the kind of pretty she is
That Asia is
That I'm not

She hands me the plant and the bone
I give her back Blue's part of the gift
Thank you.
I say for Blue
Already slack jaw slobbering
You can give it to him if you want.
She unwraps the bone and offers it to Blue
He gently takes it
Knowing better
Than to grab

The smell of meat grease fills the air
As Blue lies down at my feet and starts to gnaw
Kierra rolls the plastic wrap into a ball between her fingers
I should offer to take it
Throw it away
But I don't
It's oily
Too greasy

I set the violet on the coffee table
Wondering how long
I'll be able to keep
Such a delicate plant alive

MINE

Blue freezes midchew
Cocks his head
An orange pickup
Pulls up the drive

It's Cody.
I say
To her
To Blue
To no one in particular

My boyfriend.
I add
Without knowing
Why

Some girls do that
Make sure everyone knows
Who their boyfriend is
But I don't
At least I didn't
Until now

Cody steps out of the cab
I wave at him
And feel kind of stupid
Because it's one of those fingertip waves
That I never do

His smile pushes that dimple into his left cheek
As he waves back
I'm glad he's here
Almost wish he wasn't
Not yet, anyway
It would just be easier
If she were
Gone

Cody takes the porch steps two at a time
Pushes open the door
Blue pops to his feet
Dashes over to show off his bone
"How're you, Scarface?"
Cody runs his hands up and down Blue's back
"He looks like he's feeling good."
He is, I say tilting my face to catch the kiss he lays on my cheek.
Kierra, Cody, Cody, Kierra.

Cody pulls off his ball cap
Tucks it under his arm
    a habit of his I loved
    until now
"Nice to meet you. Did you just move here?"
Kierra tucks a strand of hair behind her ear
Looks at the couch
I'm still standing
So she does too

She looks out the front window
Hard
Like she's forgotten something

Lost it somewhere past the glass
"Me and my sister are staying with my grandma Jean until my
    dad gets here."

Which really isn't an answer
Not that Cody seems to care
"Really? That's great! I mean, your grandma's place is right
    down from my family's."
Sweet and polite, let's make it right time is over
Two steps left and I'm standing
Next to Cody
Mr. Welcome-to-the-Neighborhood
That's not even his real smile
This goofy grin he's giving her

What's wrong with him?
I wish I didn't know

ALMOST

Cody's turning me into one of
Those girls
Who pout
Every time their boyfriend
Talks
To another girl

This isn't who I want to be
But I am
At least right now

Hey.
"Hey, what?"
His eyes wander out the door
After her

"I was just being nice. She's new."
Whatever.
"Are you jealous? You know I love you."
Cody closes his eyes
Smooches his lips
A cartoon-style lip-smack kiss

My throat's getting tighter and tighter
Like it does before I cry
Not that I
Do that often
I hate
To cry

Blue lies down
Across my feet
Starts to chew on his bone
My dog
With the stitches and staples
Holding together the hurt
That could have been a gone
A forever gone
Like they always are

My voice is quiet
Tight
She practically killed my dog.
Cody's eyes go wide
"I was just messing around. You know I wouldn't ever—"

Leave you.
Is how the sentence would end
If I let it
But I don't
I'm sorry. I know you wouldn't.

He smiles
The real kind
And hugs me tight
I press my face into his shoulder

Pull away
As Blue stands
Gives me
The look
And relocates to his bed

Next to the couch
To chew on his bone
In peace

We follow him over
Curl into each other
On the couch
Cody fishes the remote from between the cushions
Turns on the television
Looks for a movie
That will make us
Laugh

Cody doesn't even know that he almost lied to me
He did, though
Everyone leaves
So he shouldn't say he won't

TIPPING POINT

It's hard to say
Why
I do it now

Why
I pull the scale
From under the trash can
Beside the toilet

Maybe
Because I haven't been hungry
Lately

Maybe if I was one of those girls
Who obsessed over magazines with more pictures than words
With shiny images of models
In white feather wings

Maybe if I was one of those girls
The number on the scale
Would matter

If I was one of those girls
I'd care
But I'm not
So I don't

Since it doesn't matter
    really it doesn't

I pull it from beneath the trash can
And step
Off a cliff
On to the scale

THE MORNING AFTER

It's usually cereal
Never toast
But sometimes an egg
First thing in the morning

I've never been one
To skip
Breakfast

But the thing is
I'm just not
Hungry

Truly

It has nothing to do
With that number
On the scale
Because really
It wasn't (was) that bad

It would just be better
If it were less

TRAMPLE AND SAMPLE

It's my job
To regulate the heat
Blowing through the vents
As Asia pulls down our drive
Onto the road
On our way to school

I grab the bandanna
Lying in the middle of the seat
To wipe the condensation
That fogs the middle of the windshield
The one place the defroster can't seem to reach

That's when I see them
Standing off to the side of the road
The part of their herd
That leaned the fence down
Wandered out of the pasture
Round behind Asia's house
Standing with their tails to the wind
Their mouths to the ground
Eating the garden bare

"We are going to be so late," Asia says.
As she pulls off the road
Again
Only this time
Headed down their drive

Asia's mom comes flying out the back door
In her mud boots and coveralls
Just as we pull in
"Hurry up, girls!"
Our hoods go back on
We're out in the rain
Chasing around in the mud
"Hey! Hey!"
Our voices mix together
As we slip slide through the tangle
Of cows
Munching on the winter vegetables coming up in rows

"Where's Cow?" Asia calls.
"I don't know. I let him out this morning and he isn't back yet,"
    her mom says.
Asia's hanging back now
Letting her mom and I get in with the herd
Oh, how I hate to deprive her of this fine opportunity
I slap at the one of the cows' hindquarters
Dodging its tail
Which flicks rain and mud at me

Asia's mom starts slapping too
But they don't even raise their heads
My hood falls off
As I run to an old red cow
Fan my hands in front of her eyes
Her head comes up fast
A clod of dirt flies through the air
From Asia's direction
Sticks to the cow's back

"Asia! That is not helping! Stop throwing and get in here!" her
    mom yells.

Another clod of dirt flies through the air
Misses the cow
Thunks
Between my shoulder blades
I spin around
More than halfway to mad

Asia squeals
Laughs
Knows what's coming her way
As I lean down and scoop up a ball of sod

She takes off
Turns to run
Not thinking about the way the mud will skid
Beneath her heels
She goes down hard
Right on her butt

I shouldn't
Let the ball of sod fly
But I do
I miss
What with laughing so hard

"Girls!" Asia's mom shouts.
Because really we aren't helping
That much

Anymore
Laughing and throwing and slipping around in this mud

Then Cow
Comes out of nowhere
Like cattle dogs do
Barking and nipping at the herd's heels
Asia's mom starts working him with whistles
"You girls better get going. You're going to be late."

My hair is so wet that I don't even bother to pull my hood up
Asia and I jog back to the truck
"Truce?" Asia slows alongside me.
Truce, I agree.
Faux serious
Offering my hand

She goes to duck
Too slow
My muddy fingers smear streaks across her cheek
Starting all over again
This laughing and throwing and slipping around in the mud

WARNING BELL

Kierra was the first person I saw this morning
When I got to school
Stepping into the middle of the year
Easy as if she's gone to school here forever
Which she hasn't
Until today

Leaning against her locker
Looking like 4th-of-July Barbie
In her freshly creased jeans
And a red button-down shirt
Laughing at Cody standing with his weight shifted to one leg
The other at a jaunty angle

Flying in through the front doors
Late after the clothes change that came after penning the cows
That had trampled and sampled Asia's mom's garden flat
Before spilling into the road

Maybe if I hadn't been so late
Running in with my blood already thumping in my chest
I wouldn't have cared
About them
Laughing
Over the joke I didn't hear

Maybe if I hadn't been so late
I wouldn't have thrown my backpack into my locker
The books raining down from the top shelf

Sending papers fluttering across the hall where they were
　　ripped and muddied
Because no one bothered to look down
To see what their heels were grinding

Maybe if I hadn't pulled away from Cody
When he leaned down to help
Ducked in for a kiss
That ended up as a mouth full of hair
When I spun away

Maybe if I hadn't slammed my locker door shut
Let Asia grab my elbow
Pull me down the hall
I would have heard what he said
Before the warning bell drowned his voice

But I don't care
I said it out loud, so Asia could hear it too
I don't care.
"What do you mean you don't care? He should have been
　　standing at your locker waiting for you, not talking to her,"
　　Asia says. "And since when does she go here anyway?"

I look back
Only this time Cody's gone
We'd been standing right across from his first period class
I'll see him second block
But still
It would have been nice if he'd waited
Just for a minute

SECOND BLOCK

Is too early for precalculus
Too soon for me to have to confront Cody
The tardy bell bleats as I step into the classroom
This room smells stagnant
Like a fish tank
Which is odd
Because Mr. Kraftner has never had one in here

Cody smiles across the room at me
Like nothing happened this morning
Him sitting there
Legs stretched out into the aisle
I wonder if it did

"Are you okay?" he asks.
I slide into the desk next to his
Sure. Why?
My books and binder come out of my bag and onto my desk
"Because you looked like you were mad this morning. I was
    going to go after you to see, but I didn't want to be late. One
    more tardy and I'll have detention."
Right.
My throat tightens around the word
"See, you are mad. I can tell from your voice."
No I'm not.

Mr. Kraftner springs from behind his luxury-liner, teacher-sized
    desk

Overflowing with coffee cups and books
He reminds me of that guy on the popcorn commercials
The one who wears a bow tie
And little Grandpa glasses
So hap-hap-happy!
Mr. Kraftner paces in front of the classroom
Thumbing through his copy of our precalculus textbook
"Pair up and let's do this! Section four, unit two. The more you
    get done in class, the less homework you have."

Cody slides his desk into place so it's facing mine
"It's because I was talking to Kierra, isn't it?"
No.
But that taste of bile in the back of my throat won't let me deny it
Even to myself

"Because if you are, you shouldn't be," Cody continues.
    "Kierra's the one who came up to me."
Which doesn't make it better
The fact that she
Came up to him

"She didn't know where her first block was."
Cody opens his textbook
Flips through the pages
Until he finds it
Section four, unit two
"I would hate starting at a new school in the middle of the
    year."
Cody's eyes fall back to his text

My heart flinches
Here I am
I'm doing it again
Turning into that girl

The kind I hate
Who cries and whines
When her boyfriend talks to another
Girl

We've been together
A year
Known each other
Forever
And I've always been
Fine

Really I don't mind
Him talking
To another
Any other
Girl

Just not her

TURN AND BURN

You can tell what horses have been worked over the winter
Whose folks had indoor arenas
With metal roofs that held the snow out
But not the wind
That blew cold through the walls

Or the people like me and Asia
Who'd pretended we didn't notice
The snow freezing to our eyelashes
Or the balls of ice packing hard in our horses' hooves
As we loped through interminable months of gray
Counting the days until the earth
Frozen silent
Beneath a crust of ice
Was released by the warmth of spring

Signaling the start of rodeo season
Team practices
Leaving the horses that had passed the winter
Standing in pastures
With their eyes blinked shut to the cold and their tails to the wind
Huffing and lathered

Sitting with my left leg dangling over Fancy's neck
Curled at the knee around the pommel
Of the saddle with the rough-out seat
Worn soft by my mom
Smooth under me
Asia and I watch

Critique
Compare
Barrel racers
Teammates

One at a time
Horses dance sideways through the gate
Into the arena
Champing at the sweet metal of their copper bits
Exploding past
Riders laid flat against their horses' necks
Breaking the stare of the electric eye
Setting the clock in motion
As they fly around the three-leaf clover

I'm on deck
Next to go
Glancing across the arena
At the road pounded into washboards by the trucks and trailers
Bumper pulls
   Goosenecks
         filing into the fairgrounds—our grounds
         except for that one week a year
         when the Tilt-a-Whirl spins people so hard and fast
         they throw their heads back
         looking at the stars twirled into a kaleidoscope
         making them think they could be anything
         go anywhere
         somewhere that wasn't born into them
         like here

Hoping to see Cody
Pulling his grandpa's blue-and-white two-horse trailer
Just as rusted and dented as the orange truck he'll be driving
With Micah slouched in the passenger seat
Staring into the side mirror at the trailer
Bouncing and swaying as one of the horses
Micah's horse
The color of a chocolate bar
Thumps his hooves against the trailer floor
At the road jouncing the trailer beneath him

But I don't

Show 'em Asia's grinning
As I swing my legs back into my stirrups
Nudging Fancy awake with my heels
Laughing as she stretches
First one hind leg
    then the other
Before walking slowly
A leisurely equine iconoclast
Into the ring
Mr. Bradford

A Mister because he's our coach
Because even if you're only three years out of high school
You're a Mister in Salida Springs
Chuckling and shaking his head at Fancy standing quiet
Not feeling her muscles
Quivering
Gathering energy beneath the saddle
Like I do

Cumulus clouds roll across the sky
Gathering
Static electricity
Gathering
Building
Gathering
Cracking across the sky
Into the arena
Ears pinned
Digging in and around the first
                        second
                              third barrel
With the wind pulling tears from my eyes

Patting Fancy's neck on our way out of the arena
Proud without even knowing our time because she's run her
   all-out best
Same as she does every time
Even when the barrels bounce off my shin and into the dirt
Still giving me her all-out best

MY COMPETITION

I stick out my hand
Slapping Asia luck as she and Scuba prance past into the arena
Scuba's eyes rolling wild
Flicking saliva onto his shoulders and neck
Already dark with sweat
Tossing his head
Trotting in place
A rocking horse on springs

My attention diverted
By the appearance of an orange truck
With three people
In the cab
Where two should have been

I wave as Cody steps out of the truck
Wondering if Asia
Trotting out of the arena
Saw Micah offering his hand to help Kierra out of the truck
Kierra
Not even bringing a horse of her own

Asia gestures in their direction
And I follow her over
To where they're unloading their horses
Tacked up and ready to go
In roping saddles
With horns the size of saucers

If Asia noticed Micah helping
Kierra
She doesn't care
Leaning off her horse and dropping into Micah's arms
Caught like a bride being carried across the threshold
Micah spins around
Swinging Asia's head under Scuba's chin
Laughing as Scuba nuzzles her forehead with his Silly Putty lips

I lean off my saddle
Back curved in a question mark
To kiss Cody
Standing beside me
Running his hand up my leg
Pushing the jealousy away

As Kierra
Aware that she turned four into five
Explains
In words coming out too fast
about how her horse is lame, sore after a bad trim. But her
grandma thought she should come out anyway. At least
watch a practice. Maybe make some friends.

Looking at Cody I know how it happened
Kierra's grandma calling Cody's mom
Living just down the road and all
If you could give her a ride
It would be such
A help

Even with Cody's hand on my leg pushing back the jealousy
I smile
When Kierra
Thanks Cody and Micah for the ride
And jogs across the parking lot to where girls she knows
Her ride home
Wave to her

COOL DOWN

I usually love this
The part that comes after
When it's just Asia and me
Pulling the tack off our horses
Tied to the side of the trailer

Tossing waves over our shoulders
At our teammates
Driving slower on the way out
Than they did on the way in
Knowing that there will be chores
And homework
Waiting for them
At home

But tonight is different
Because my mind keeps sliding back
To Kierra
And what I want to ask Asia
Is this
How can you not care about
Her
Showing up
With them

Scuba's hindquarters swing wide
As he sidesteps away from Asia's shoulder
Into me
Stop it!

I say as I trip into Fancy
Bouncing off one horse and into another
Neither one interested enough to lift their heads
From the hay
They're teasing from the rope feeders
Dangling from the trailer windows

"You aren't even listening to me."
Asia drapes her arms over Scuba's back
Scratching his withers as she talks
"We've got to make it to Nationals this year."
Knowing she isn't just talking about going
She's talking about winning
Barrels and poles
Maybe goat tying
Winning All-Around

We might be juniors
But she doesn't want
To wait
Until our senior year
To bring that saddle home

All I care about is barrels though
I want to win
That event
Not at Silver State
But at Nationals
        just like my mom

I pull a hoof pick out of my back pocket
Left hand down Fancy's leg

Her hoof in my hand
Sinking the pick into the arena dirt
Packed hard
Around her frog
Against her sole
Focusing hard
On scraping it clean
Because all it takes is a single stone
To leave a bruise

I feel like Fancy and I have plateaued. I'm not sure what to do
   about our time.
"Have you thought about your saddle?"
What about it?
"It looked like you were riding kind of high."
High?
"Like maybe you need to go up a size. What is it? A fourteen-
   inch?"
I'm not sure. Maybe.
Definitely

Focus
      Focus
            Focusing on Fancy's hoof
Because I don't want to look at Asia
When I feel myself melting
Inside

"I mean, you're tiny, but you should check. A bigger saddle
   and you'd be sitting a little deeper."
A bigger saddle
Or a smaller me

You're right. I probably should.
"Any little bit helps."

Which I know
Is true

JUST THINK ABOUT IT

"Would it be stupid if I tried out for court this year?"
Asia flicks on the headlights
Glances into the rearview mirror at the horse trailer
As the road changes from asphalt
To dirt
Alerting us that we're halfway
Home

It would be stupid if you didn't.
It still throws me
When Asia asks questions like this
Genuinely not seeing
That she would be the perfect
Most obvious
Choice
To represent our state
As the rodeo queen
At Nationals

"You should do it too! Try out with me!"
No way.
"Please! It would be so much fun if we did it together!"
I hate and I love this about her
The two wound tight
The fact that she thinks
I should even be a
Choice

"Think about the scholarship."
Which would be nice
Amazing actually
"And you know you want to wear a sparkly tiara."
Because the funny thing is
I actually used to

Asia and I had matching crowns
When we were little
Plastic tiaras with pastel stones
We'd get her dad to throw hay bales
From the loft
Down to the barn floor
Walls for our alfalfa castles

They could never find tiaras as nice as the ones we used to have.
"So true. But still, you have to try out with me."
I'm just not—
"Rae, don't even start. You are adorable."
Cute as a button.

I bat my eyes and shrug my shoulders
Topping it off with a cuter than cute smile
Because the only thing more uncomfortable
Than feeling less than attractive
Is having someone tell you
You're pretty

"Stop," Asia laughs.
I slip my feet out of my boots
Tucking my foot under my leg
As I pull my hair back

Twirling it into
A knot

"You look like her, you know."
We don't do this very often
Talk about my mom
That's what my dad says.
"Because you do."

I wish
I think
Knowing that there are plenty of girls who would cringe
If you told them they looked like
Their moms
But maybe that's because they didn't have one
As perfect
As mine

I miss her.
My right hand slides around
To my back
Tracing my vertebrae
Three
    Two
One

"Me too." Asia says
They would feel wrong
Those words
If they'd come
From anyone
But her

Because no one
Not even my Dad
Misses her
Like me

But it's Asia
And me
So it's all right to let them sit
Those words
Between us
For the rest of the ride
Home

INTENTION

A buck five
With her boots on
That's what my dad would always say
When he was describing
My mom

Which would explain
Her saddle
The one she rode
Passed on to me

Fits Fancy so nice
Used to fit me too
And it will
Again

Once I whittle
That number
On the scale
Down

Which won't be hard
Since I haven't been
Hungry
Lately

It won't be hard
Now
That I have

A goal

Smaller
Leaner
Lighter
In the saddle

It won't be hard
Because I'm willing to do
Whatever
It takes

To win

DADDY'S LITTLE GIRL

I cook for Dad most every night
Tuesdays are special though
Daughter-dad night
Even when Mom was still alive
Before purple and black rivers of bruises
Ran up and down her arms
Where the needles
Delivering medicine more toxic than the cancer
Pricked her tissue-paper skin

Tuesday was our night to eat whatever we felt like making
Eggs on waffles drowned in maple syrup
Purple Cow milkshakes with grape juice and vanilla ice cream
Fries dunked in ranch dressing
Laughing over whatever movie I picked to watch

Now we watch those "reality" shows
Both groaning over the ridiculous characters
The nonexistent plotlines

We can't turn them off
These Tuesday nights
When I lean up against my dad on the couch
Allowing myself to be his little girl

MY WRONG TO RIGHT

Sitting with my feet propped on Blue's back
At the kitchen table
I pore over the charts in the cookbooks
Listing calories, nutrients, fat
Because dinner tonight
The first Tuesday Dad's been home all month
        what with the cattle
        and the work
It has to be
Right

I look over the cookbooks
Through the sliding glass door at Fancy
And the goats we ended up with after last week's sale at the
    stockyard
Two yellow-white nanny goats with nubs for ears
Wearing green nylon collars
Frayed at the ends
One with a bell
One without

Milk goats
Left standing in a pen on top of a hay bale molded black
They'd nosed Dad's hand through the fence while he was
    talking to cattle buyers
Leftovers
Too old to be sold
Can't run broken-down nanny goats through the ring at the end
    of a sale

Not like butcher cows
Even with their cancer eyes and prolapsed uteruses
Their insides dangling dead and rank
Those cows are worth something

So Dad brought the goats home
Reading once that every race horse gets a goat
A buddy to keep them company in their stall
Might as well give Fancy some buddies too
Who doesn't need a friend?
He'd reasoned

I'm jealous of the goats
Standing easy and natural in the grass
Alongside their equine companion
I hope it comes that easy to me and Dad tonight
Like it has always been
Was
Before the spaces
Holes
Started opening between us
I can't remember when it was
That they appeared

The problem is that I can't eat everything
Not like I used to
The smell of fat
Of grease
Stays on my fingers
Coating my stomach
Making it impossible to sleep

But I can't think about that
Flipping through the pages of the cookbooks with the pictures
   of food
On white china and woven place mats
Breaking up the columns of measurements
Ingredients
Chopped pureed minced pressed kneaded
Into a succulent whole

Tonight I am going to make up for the nights when I
Forgot to
Had already
Eaten

Tonight
I won't
Forget

RAIN CHECK

Dad had to work
Straight through the day and into the night
Ringy cows wouldn't load
Raced across the mesa with their heads in the air

I'd finally decided what I was going to make
Pizza
His favorite
Heavy with meat and American cheese
His side
Veggies
No cheese
On mine

But it's okay
He didn't make it home
I hadn't even started cooking when he called
I'd been standing in the kitchen
Staring into the refrigerator
Ignoring the sun melting red and gold behind the barn
Listening to Blue crunching his kibbles
Tags chinging off the edge of his metal food dish
When the phone had rung

"I'm so sorry. I'll have to take a rain check. Go ahead and eat
     without me," he'd said.
I understand, Dad.
We'll do it again.
Next week.

It's okay
Really
It
Is

TOPOGRAPHY

He walked through the front door
Shed his coat and boots
That filled the house with the smell of cattle
Went straight to the shower
I figured I might as well too
Only for me
A bath

A mountain range
That looks a lot like my knees
Streaming glaciers of bubble bath suds
Pops up in front of me

Blue's legs twitch
Chasing cattle across a dreamscape
Stretched out on the duck-shaped bath mat
That reminds me of bathtub toys
And the shampoo hairdos I used to get
Back when bathing was an event

I'd sit princess proud in our claw-footed tub
Wrapped in the steamy air
That smelled like plastic strawberries,
As Mom twirled my little-kid hair into spikes and curls

This is the part I hate
The getting out part
I always do it fast

Grab a towel and wrap it around my middle
Before I even step out of the tub and over Blue

Blue stretches out of his nap
Annoyed into consciousness by my feet
Leaving watermarks
On the rubber duck rug
As I whisk the towel over my
Arms, back, legs

He lumbers out of the bathroom and into my room
Chooses a tangle of T-shirts on the floor in the corner
    for a dog bed
        turns once
            twice
          three times a charm
His mouth falls open into a yawn
Run through with a whine
As he flops back into his nap

I look out my bedroom window
Where the moon has swallowed the sun
The stars poke through the dark
Reminding me how late it is
As I shove my legs into my pajamas

I pull a sweatshirt over my head
Wondering
Hoping
Dad's still awake

Maybe
We can talk
Watch TV
Or
Something
Because I've missed him
On these nights
He's been gone

I've missed him
A lot

WHAT IF

Our house breathes
In creaks and groans at night
Even my moccasin slippers
Make the stairs complain
As Blue and I walk down and
Into the living room
Where I find Dad
Asleep
On the couch

He says it's more comfortable than his bed
When his back is tired
After a day of driving
Dad's arms are crossed
With his hands
Pressing the book
He must have been reading
To his chest

The woodstove is going
But he still might get cold later
So I grab the ivory-and-blue blanket off the rocking chair
Drape it across him
Dad snuffle snores
As I click off the reading lamp
Shining down on the couch

I wonder if this is what Dad looked like
When he and Mom first met

The creases around his eyes and mouth
Relaxed smooth
High school sweethearts
Like Cody and me

We don't ever talk
About what we'll be
After college
Cody plus me
Without me
I try not to think about it
But sometimes I wonder

Blue winds around the coffee table
Goes to nose Dad's arm
Blue, I whisper. *Let Daddy sleep.*
My fingertips find my collarbone
A bite-my-nails kind of habit
That never keeps the fluttering that fills my throat away
When I think about
Blue.
He cocks his head at my whisper
Follows me back up the stairs

Mom used to say that to me
When Dad would fall asleep in the living room
"Let your daddy sleep. He works so hard. We have to let him
    rest whenever we can."
It always made me feel so grown-up
Giving Dad the break he hardly ever let himself take
But I don't know why it came out now
Just the way she used to say it

He's not Daddy
He's Dad now

The stairs aren't cooperating
They're creaking so loud I stop
My fuzzy shadow freezes too
Let Daddy sleep
Repeat rewind over and over in my head
What if I had woken him
The night after she came home from the hospital

I look at the pictures
Running up and down the wall
Alongside the stairs
Pictures of her and me on her red roan mare
Before I was even old enough to walk
She and Dad and I standing in the ocean the summer I was six
I hadn't known where we were going for our vacation that year
Until the day before we left
I'd come down to breakfast
Found a metal sand pail
Full of starfish-shaped sand molds
With a picture of the sea taped to the side

What if, I whisper.
She's not going back
Dad had told me
And I'd known what that meant
Mom should have been better
Because the breast cancer was gone
That's what the doctors had told us anyway
But it was her heart

Sick from the drugs
That were supposed to keep her well
Keep her here

That last night
I hadn't woken Daddy up
Not with him being so tired
Let Daddy sleep
Mom would have been proud
But I should have known
I should have woken him up
                    because
                        maybe
                            if I had
                            he could have helped
                            stopped the inevitable
                            and we would have had
                            one more night
                            with her

MONARCH WINGS

I was there when she died
I'd crept across the hall
Barefoot
Into her bedroom
Where I'd stood
Next to Dad
Crumpled in sleep
In the rocking chair by her bed

I'd listened to her breath rattling in her lungs
Like leaves
Browned and brittle
Chased down the sidewalk by a jagged breeze

I'd caught a tear with my pinky
As it fell from my eye
And laid it on her cheek

I'd set one hand on Dad's arm
And placed the other on her wrist
Where a Monarch's wings fluttered beneath my fingertips

I'd pulled the quilt back and slid into bed beside her
Careful not to disturb her sleep
I wrapped my arms around her
Counting the spaces between her breaths
Each one longer then the next

When the sunlight pried Dad's eyes open
That's what he saw
Me curled on my side
Pressed into Mom
Breathing for us both

INCREMENTALLY

There's nothing drastic
About what I'm
Going to
Do

Minus five
Will simply mean
Smaller
Leaner
Lighter
Faster in a sport
Where every tenth of a second
Counts

So now
As long as I'm awake
Not that I ever really went to sleep
Even after Dad got home
What with my mind being so busy
Thinking about
My lunch

Standing at the kitchen counter
I pack my lunch
As the sun creeps over the horizon
Leaking slivers and swirls
Of yellow and orange
Across the sky

Carrots first
Into a Ziploc bag
Red pepper
Celery
Snow peas
Each into another
Some crackers
Just for show
Because the veggies
They're all I'll eat

I drop them all
Into my lunch sack
Tabulating the calories
Adding
Up the numbers
That will equal
That number
On the scale
Minus
Five

WORLD GEOGRAPHY

It's the three of us
Cody
        Asia
And me
At a table built for four
In the classroom papered with maps
Where we should be working on our geography presentation
About the country
Of our
Choice

"I think we should consider asking her," Asia's saying.
But I hear
Only the sound of my heart
Thrumming
Of my dog
Crying
"Oh, do you?" Cody quips in a faux professor brogue.
"I do," Asia says.
Not that I care
That they want to ask
Her

Not that I care
That she and Asia are now closer than close
Study partners
In Spanish
Where I take it they talk
About more than their assignments

"We need to elect a new secretary since Jaycee moved and she's
  the best choice."
Why? She hasn't even practiced with us yet.
Not even trying to dull the edge
My voice gets
When I'm as annoyed
As this

"That doesn't matter. I mean, I obviously wouldn't ask her to
  run—"
    Asia pauses here
    double-check
    checking to make sure I heard the way her voice dipped
    at the
        obviously
    best friend alliance signified
"But we need someone with her fund-raising experience."
"Wasn't Kierra the president of the rodeo team at her last
  school?"
How does he even know this?
Cody, who can hardly remember Asia is our club's president
  and Micah's our vice
    "Yes, and she helped put together a mammoth auction
        that pulled in all the money they needed for their entire
        rodeo."
"That'd be nice," Cody says.
    "We could do it too. One or two big fund-raisers instead of
        a bunch of little ones," Asia says. "I felt like I was a first-
        grader selling candy bars last year."
"That was the most expensive fund-raiser ever," Cody sighed.

I'd almost forgotten
How Cody had eaten an entire case of chocolate bars
Before he had even realized it
One here
Another there
Promising to pay himself back
Until suddenly
They were gone

My throat goes tight
Thinking about
Streaks of
    butter
        oil
    fat
Along the edges of the chocolate wrappers

"We're still doing the car washes though, aren't we?"
Cody wraps his arm around my shoulders
Grins at me big
As he pulls me close
"They're my favorite."

No
    No
No
Stomps through my mind
My stomach clenches at the thought
Of putting
On a bikini
Even just the top
With a pair of shorts

Like Asia and I did last year
Dancing around on the sidewalk
Waving cardboard and Sharpie signs
Pulling rigs off the road and into the high school parking lot
For the rest of the team to scrub
Because whose truck doesn't need
A wash and a shine?

"Stop being such a guy," Asia says. "I'm serious. We need to
    talk her into running. I'm not selling candy bars again."
Asia pauses
Raises her eyebrows at me and Cody
"Unless one of you two wants to run."
Which isn't fair
She knows neither of us will
Because we're selfish like that
Refusing to focus on anything
But our events

"No, Kierra would be perfect," Cody says.
Perfect.
I repeat
Because as much as I hate the idea
Of Kierra
In the position
I'm not going to run

"That's what I thought."
Asia presses the eraser end of her pencil against her forehead
As she leans closer to the textbook
Spread open between us
"Japan," she says. "We should definitely do Japan."

The topic of Kierra
Open-shut-closed
For them
Not for me
How can I let it rest when—

"We should," Cody agrees.
He slaps his hand against the table
"Sushi! Think of the extra credit we'd get if we bring in sushi!"
Asia rolls her eyes
Attempts to pull me into the joke Cody wasn't trying to make
But really
"How could we make sushi?" Asia asks. "Where are we getting
    raw fish?"
"I don't know. I'm just saying, if we did, we'd probably get an A."

"That's all you then, Cody. See if you can round up some raw
    fish."
Asia glances at the clock
Twelve minutes
Until
Lunch
Her cue to say
"I'm so hungry."
Because she says it every day at this time

Leaner
Lighter
Faster
I think about my goal
Minus five

Me too.
Wondering when I became
This good
At telling
Lies

PICTURE PERFECT

I doubt she needed an invitation
But she got one
From Asia

A quick wave and a smile
Tossed across the cafeteria
Was all it took
To bring her
Over

To stand between us
Balancing a stack of library books in one arm
Her lunch tray in the other
Featuring today's cafeteria special
A BLT and fries

Deep fat fryer fries
Sweating shadows of grease
Through their paper tray
How can she eat them
And still be so thin?

"Didn't you elect officers last spring?" Kierra asks.
"Yes, but Jaycee moved, so we're short a secretary."
"Nobody will vote for me," Kierra says.
"They will," Asia says. "Trust me."

Thumbs to my hip bones
I can feel them

Through my jeans
But they should be
Will be
Sharper
Soon

"Just think about it, okay?" Asia says.
"I will."
Kierra picks up the conversation
Spins it from Asia to me
"How's Blue?"
I hate that she asked
Would have raged if she hadn't
I wish she would go
Good.
"I'm so glad."

"Hey, Kierra," Cody says.
As he and Micah materialize
Emerging from the lunchroom crowd to
Sliding into their spots at the table
Across from Asia and me

Back from chasing down drinks
Because it seemed like such a waste
For all of us to stand in line at the vending machines
"Sorry, but they were out of Sprite," Micah says.
As he slides a Sierra Mist across the table to Asia
Nods a greeting to Kierra

Cody hands me
A Diet Coke

"I don't know why you drink that. All the chemicals are so
         much worse for you than the sugar in this," Cody says as
         he pops open his Coke.

There's something about the chemical taste that I like
It feels cleaner
Lighter
Than the corn syrup sweetness
That would leave my throat thick
If I drank a regular Coke

Kierra is still standing
I don't know why
"Grab a seat," Cody suggests.
Kierra smiles at him
Looks at me
"Thanks, but Morgan is waiting for me."
"Let me know what you decide," Asia says.
"Okay, I will."
Plan confirmed
Kierra slips away

I turn the Diet Coke can
Slick and cold
In my hand
Read the panel on the side
Nutrition Facts
Zero
     Zero
          Zero

ATTENTION DIVERTED

I want to say something
Snide
But Asia's distracted
Unpacking the almond butter and honey sandwich
She brings every day
Eyeing the Oreos
Micah is pulling out of his lunch sack
Too busy to notice me
Watching her

"That's sweet that she does that, isn't it?" Cody says.
Watching Kierra sitting across from her cousin now
A freshman who struggles
With everything
Especially math
After coming off his quad
Hitting his head
Last year
Their calculators are out
She's sorting through his binder for him
As he thumbs through his textbook

"So sweet," Micah says in a little girl voice.
Cody punches his shoulder, "Well, it is."
Micah punches him back
Barely nicking his ribs
Asia leans across the table and swipes Micah's Oreos
"Want one?" she offers.

No thanks.
There's an empty space on the table
In front of me
That needs to be filled
Before more offers come
I reach into my lunch sack and pull out
The red pepper
    snow peas
        celery
    carrots

"That better not be your whole lunch," Asia says.
Why?
"Because that's not a lunch."
"Unless you're a rabbit," Cody volunteers.

Micah ducks under our words
Across the table
Makes a grab for his Oreos
Sending Cody's pop rolling across the table
Spewing Coke into Asia's lap

"Micah!" Asia jumps up
Saves her sandwich
Just in time
Cody and Micah throw their napkins at the puddle
Growing into a lake
I run and grab some more

By the time I'm back
Asia is in the restroom
Cleaning up

Cody and Micah are still wiping
The table dry

I finish cleaning up
Slide the soppy napkins
Onto an empty tray
Someone has left behind

I take it to the trash
Along with my lunch
Where I
Toss
It
All
Glancing up at the clock on the cafeteria wall
As the warning bell bleats

Seven minutes and counting
Until I have my next class
I wouldn't have had time to eat
My lunch

Even
If
I
Wanted

PASSING PERIOD

Life happens
Between the school bells

Fourth block is gone
Three
        Two
One
Minute to go and fifth block
Will be here

I stand outside the doorway
To my class
As Asia fumbles
In her bag
"I know I've got it."
Hair falling into her eyes
As she searches for the calculator
She borrowed
That I'll need

"Asia!" Kierra calls.
Pulls out of the crush
Moving through the hall
        Asia looks up
        focus gone
        "Hey, Kierra."
"Go ahead and do it. Put me on the ballot. I'll run."
"Really?" Asia looks at me
Smiles

Like Kierra just gave us
The most fabulous gift
Ever

Great.
I say
Thinking only of
My dog
    my dog
Crying

"It will be good, right? A chance to get to know more people?"
   Kierra says.
"Absolutely!"
Kierra tucks her hair behind her ear
"Is there anything I have to do?"
"Nope. Just show up for our meeting. Tomorrow. After school.
   Mr. Retsom's room."
"Thanks again for thinking of me."
"No problem."
Asia shrugs her bag onto her shoulder
Kierra slides through the door to her classroom
On the other side of the hall

The bell rings
I'm now officially late for class
"Isn't this great? Cody will be so excited, right? Now he won't
   have to sell candy bars again."
He'll be excited
About more than the candy bars
Sure. Calculator?
"Oh, right! Sorry!"

Asia pulls it out of her bag
Shoves it into my hand
And is
Gone

I glance at my calculator
Running my thumb over the plus and minus keys
As I slide into my desk

Reminding myself
That I can't let Kierra
Or anything else
Get in the way
Of my goal

    smaller
        leaner
            lighter
                faster
                like
                my
                mom

ICE-CUBE POPSICLE

I love cooking shows
All the ingredients separated into tiny glass bowls
On a counter
So large it's an island
In a kitchen big as our living room

This chef
She's my favorite
Wearing more black this season than last
When she wore lots of red
Heavier now than she was then
Not a lot
But enough
To wear black

The woodstove is chock-full of wood
Burning so hot Blue's tongue dangles
He's splayed out on the couch next to me
Like he's sunbathing
And I'm warm
For the first time all week
Cozy
In two pairs of sweats
    wool socks
        hooded sweatshirt

If Dad were home
He'd give me a bad time

About using so much wood
Because it hasn't been
That cold
Unseasonably warm
For February

But he's not here
It's just me
And Blue
Watching the perfect chef
In her perfect kitchen
Making the perfect meal

Commercial break
I catapult
Off the couch
Into motion
    jumping jacks—running-in-place—high knees—football
      shuffle—running-in-place—heels to butt
    up and down the stairs—once-twice-three times with
      Blue at my heels—skidding across the linoleum in the
      kitchen—snake an ice-cube Popsicle from the freezer

And return to our regularly scheduled programming
To sit cross-legged on the couch
Licking an ice-cube Popsicle
Watching
The perfect chef
In her perfect kitchen
Making the perfect meal

That neither she
Or I
Will eat

SCHIZO

When the night falls open
Eclipsing the day
The monologue
Begins

Recounting the moments that
Could have
Should have
Been
If only I would have
Could have
Done this
Said that

Listening to this monologue
Detailing
Everything that should have happened, but didn't
The day that should have been
But wasn't
Because I didn't
Hadn't been able to
Frown then
Laugh when

This must be what it's like to be schizophrenic
Your internal world
Your mind
Crowded and consumed

SECOND TIME THIS WEEK

I swore I wouldn't do it again
Swore on my mother's grave
This
Again

It doesn't matter though
My best intentions
Evanescent

I'm sick
I'm weak
My throat burns from the bile
I wish it hurt more

Penance
     jump rope
Penance
     jumping jacks
Penance
     more jumping jacks

It's not fast enough, not hard enough, not enough

In the bathroom
I rinse my mouth
Raise my eyes to the medicine cabinet
Cold sweat
Shivering

The mirror is a pond
My image
Floats
On its surface
The weight of the water
Still and dark
Beckons

I fall

A.M. ROUTINE

The number
Didn't go down
It didn't go up
But it didn't go down
It should have
After last night

The linoleum is cold under my bare feet as I step off the scale
So I step back on
Same number

My clothes are folded square
Stacked on top of the toilet lid
Only I forgot to grab socks from my dresser
Which means I'll have to run
To my bedroom when I'm dressed
My feet freezing
Which makes me mad

And my face
Looks fat
My legs
Are fat
Not that I care
Because maybe if I weren't so weak
I wouldn't be
So fat

It's just that my
Feet
Are turning to ice on the bathroom floor
And I can't shove
My legs
Into my jeans fast enough
Or my arms
Into my shirt quick enough
Because I'm so fucking cold

I move fast fast fast out of the bathroom
Into my room
Where I ram my toe into a stack of books on the floor
Spin away on one foot
Hopping tripping over these fucking books
That I send flying

"You okay up there?" Dad calls.
Yeah, I just tripped.
Only Blue knows better
Standing on the opposite side of the bed
Staring at me

I hate myself for not remembering
That he always waits for me
Curled in a fuzzy dog ball
While I get ready for school

I'm so selfish that I didn't even think
About how I'd scare him awake
With those books
Flying through the air

Those books that could have hit him,
But all I ever think about is me

I crawl over the bed and kneel on the floor next to him
His body doesn't bend into the hug I give him
So I take his face in my hands
He looks
Over my shoulder

I'm sorry, buddy.
A micro tail wag
I say it again

He sideswipes me with his tongue
All is forgiven
At least on his part anyway

RAINSTORM

The smells float up the stairs
Waffles and sausage
Make my mouth fill with saliva
The kind that used to come when I'd get hungry
Now reminds me of getting sick
The way your mouth waterfalls cold
Just before you throw up

Blue follows me down the stairs
Into the living room
Where Asia's waiting
She and Dad are standing in the middle of the living room
Watching the news
Dad must've changed the channel when she arrived
Because he always watches cartoons in the morning
A fact nobody knows but Mom and me
Or, Mom did
Dad can't stand to start the day hearing about murders and car
    crashes

"Morning," Asia says.
Morning.
"We're just trying to find a weather report to see how long this
    rain will last."
Dad sets the remote on the coffee table
Steps out of the living room
Into the kitchen
Returns with two waffle sandwiches wrapped in napkins
Gives one to me

One to Asia too
Sausage and egg
Glued to the waffles with maple syrup and salt
Just a little bit of the salt
To go with the sweet
I used to love

Now all I can think about are the beads of
Fat
That make the sausage
Pop
Between my teeth

We walk out the door
Stop at the edge of the porch
Stand for a second
Staring into the gray mist
Melting out of the clouds

"You look tired."
Asia's not looking at me when she says it
For some reason I wish she was
Thanks.
"Sorry, I'm not trying to be mean, but you do."

The waffle sandwich is warm in my hand
The iron pressed squares cup my fingertips
As I squeeze
The layers together

"We better get going. I have to make copies before first block."
Why?

"Agendas. Rodeo club meeting. Did you forget?"
How could I?
But I had
Actually forgotten
That's the thing about nights
Like last night
    when I let the food in
    had to force it out
They wipe
Everything
Clean

Asia looks at me now
Begins her sentence with a sigh
"Please don't be weird about this."
I'm not.
"Whatever. You should cut her some slack. It was an accident,
    you know? Besides, we're doing more than electing a new
    secretary. We have a whole rodeo to plan."
Asia pulls the hood of her jacket up before she steps
Off the porch
Into the rain

I do the same
Honestly
Not meaning to let my supposed-to-be breakfast
Fall out of my hand
Onto the ground
It's an accident
You know

Asia jogs around to the driver's side of the truck
Her head bowed against the gray
She doesn't even see it happen
And I'm glad
So glad as I swing the passenger door open
Climb into the truck

I lick the syrup off my fingers
Repeating it in my head
That number
Minus five

THE LIST IS LONG

Arena Director
Announcer
Secretary
Judges
Timers
Stock Contractor
Bullfighters
Pickup riders
Just to name a few

Then there are the sponsors
For buckles
Saddles
Headstalls
Who is getting those
This year?

Asia is asking
Micah is listing
On the dry-erase board at the front of the room
As the rest of our team sits
Behind desks
In this classroom
Turned club meeting space

Then there's the issue of a fund-raiser
Hopefully singular
Not plural

Asia continues
Because as we all know
The annual Salida Springs High School Rodeo
Isn't a cheap
Affair

Kierra actually has a notebook out
Which makes me mad
(irrational I know)
But seriously
She's not even secretary
Yet

I'm not going to be
That person
The petty
Angry one
Who breaks a team
A friendship
In half

I remind myself of that
As I lean over
And take Cody's water bottle off his desk
Unscrewing the cap
Expecting water
Getting lemonade

The shock of the sugar
Calories
Hitting my throat

Makes me cough
Cody laughs
At the lemonade
Nearly coming out
My nose

"Give me that," he whispers.
Swiping it from my hand
"Raesha will take care of the sponsors," he volunteers
As I try to catch my breath
Between coughs
"Perfect," Asia says
Directing Micah
To write my name down

I kick Cody in the calf
With the heel of my boot
Because now everyone is looking at us
And laughing
Not a lot
But enough

Cody winks at me
Knowing it's my turn
To volunteer him for something
Now

None of them realizing that the only thing
Running through my mind
Are numbers
Ninety-nine calories per eight ounces
In the lemonade

I didn't mean
To swallow

MEETING ADJOURNED

I check the box
Next to her name
On the paper ballot
Micah
Handed me
The voting
The last item on the agenda
Today

Ignoring the way Asia
Is leaning into her conversation with Kierra
The two of them sitting side by side
At the front of the room
Smiling and laughing

"What are you doing after this?" Cody asks
Taking the ballot from my hand
I have to run to the feed store to pick up some vaccinations.
"Do you want me to go with you? We could get something to
　　eat afterward."
　　　I sift through his words
　　　wondering what he means by that
　　　do I look like I need to
　　　want to
　　　eat?
*I wish. I should get home. Dad's hauling cattle tonight, so I have to
　　feed.*
"All right. Your loss. I was thinking ice cream."

Cody stands and walks to the front of the room

Where Micah is collecting the ballots

"Want to go get something to eat after this?" Cody asks him.

"Sure." Micah grabs our ballots and shoves them into the shoe
   box

With the slit on top

"Want to come?" Micah asks Asia.

"Of course," Asia says. "Kierra, you should come too."

"I can't. I rode in with Morgan today and—"

"Come on. We can start brainstorming ideas for our fund-
   raiser," Asia says.

"I'll give you a ride home," Cody volunteers. "It's not like we
   live that far apart."

Leaner

Lighter

Faster

Mr. Welcome-to-the-Neighborhood is back

"You're sure you don't want to come, Raesha?" Cody asks.

I stand

Grab my bag

Well, I—

"What?" Asia says. "You don't want something to eat? That's
   a shocker."

In that tone reserved

For inside jokes

About girls we just don't

Couldn't possibly understand

What with them being

So vapid and dull

"I can't imagine you're not hungry," Asia continues.
It's not that—
Asia turns away
From the crater
I have created
Between her and me
By not needing
Wanting
To eat

So I remind myself
Of the promise I made
Not to be the person
Who breaks this friendship
This team
In half
It's fine. I can go. I'll just feed a little late.

"Then let's go," Asia says.
The gauntlet is thrown
I follow her out the door
Toward her truck
Cody, Micah, and Kierra
Right behind

BETTER LEFT UNSAID

There's a spreadsheet in my head
With columns for calories
Type of food eaten
And when

Now it's completely askew
Because I have no idea
How much lemonade
I drank

I know it's crazy
Obsessing like this
Over an ounce
Maybe four

I wish I could reach through the space
Between Asia and I
And say
Just that

But instead we walk out to her truck
Side by side
Not talking about the comments she made
The ones I'm choosing to ignore

Knowing I can't explain
All of this crazy
Going on
In my head

TINY'S HARDWARE AND MORE

Cody and Micah pull up to the curb
Asia parks
Her truck close behind

Close enough for me to see that Cody is driving
With one hand on the steering wheel
The other arm draped across the back of the seat
His hand behind
Around?
Kierra's shoulder

I tell myself that last part is only my mind
Playing tricks on me
Because Cody wouldn't
Couldn't do that
To me

"What are you getting?" Asia asks
As she turns off the ignition
Tucks her keys into the visor
I don't know.
"It better be something."
Asia slams her door
Harder than she needs to

"It's the hardware store, but they have the best ice cream in
    town," Cody is saying,
As he offers his hand to Kierra
Helping her out of the truck

That really isn't jacked up enough
To warrant
This chivalrous gesture

But I'm not going to get mad
The last thing I need
Is to look as crazy on the outside
As I feel
On the inside

What are you buying me?
I ask as I catch up to Cody
Sliding my hand into his back pocket
He wraps his arm around my waist
"Whatever you want," he says and lays a kiss on my cheek. "As
    long as you're willing to share."

I'm willing to share ice cream
But that's it
I think
Cutting my eyes at Kierra
As I step through the door
Cody is holding
For me

Asia and Micah are already inside
Side by side
In front of the freezer case
Debating
Toffee Mocha Crunch
Versus
Salted Carmel Swirl

We step into line behind them
Two plus two
And then there was one
Which makes it easier to forget
His hand on her shoulder
When she's standing
Behind us
Alone

The front door clanks open
Asia's uncle Bud steps into the store
"Now here's trouble," he says.
Giving Asia's shoulder a quick squeeze
"Hi, Uncle Bud."

"After-school ice cream?" he asks.
"Of course," Asia says.
"Well, if anyone wants to help fix fence afterward, I can put
   you to work," Bud offers.
"No thanks," Cody says.
"I'm good," Micah seconds.
"Don't say I didn't ask."

Bud laughs
Continues on his way
Heads straight to the back of the store
Where the tools
That are the biggest part of the "More"
Are kept

I was hoping there would be more talk
More back and forth

Giving me time to think
About how to handle this ice cream
Situation

My fingertips tap
                    tap
           tap
Against my sternum
As Cody guides me toward the freezer case
Arm still around my waist
"I'm a purist," he's explaining over his shoulder to Kierra.
Because I'm sure she cares
"Dutch chocolate. No toppings. The only thing I ever get," he
    says.

I scan my choices
As he talks
Wishing I knew which flavors have the most calories
Which ones have the least
I'm guessing vanilla
Hope I'm right
As I make my way to the end of the rainbow of ice cream

There are two new
"Check us out!" flavors
Raspberry and marionberry sorbet
One hundred percent fruit juice
Meaning no milk
No fat
I feel like I'm going to cry
So happy that my decision
Is made

EASY OUT

Bud emerges from the back
Fence stretcher in one hand
Wallet in the other
Pings the silver bell on the counter
Smiling toward the back door
As he lays his purchase
Next to the cash register
"What's somebody got to do to get some service around here?"

"Now what's all the commotion about?" Tiny calls
Coming in through the stockroom door behind the counter
    with Sniffles
His little red terrier
Tucked under one arm
Just as small
As Tiny is huge
"Bud. What you making all this noise for? You're going to run
    off all my customers."

Tiny hands Asia a container
Of freshly cut strawberries
"Well hello, darlin'."
"Hi, Grandpa," Asia says as she puts the container
In the empty space
On the toppings bar
Between the Oreo crumbles and the sprinkles

Tiny sets down his dog
Pulls his apron off the hook on the wall

Washes his hands in the sink opposite the freezer case
Asking after our families
As he grabs an ice cream scoop
Reminding us to keep up our grades
As he fills our cups and cones
With more ice cream
Then he should

Go ahead, Kierra, I say
Acting as if I'm still deciding
Watching as she orders not one flavor
But two
Wondering how
Why
Anyone would want to eat
All that

May I have the raspberry?
Acting like the decision is no big deal
Excited to try a new flavor
"The sorbet?" Tiny says. "Excellent choice."

Bud yawns
Stretches his arms
Cracks his back
"Keep your shirt on, Ornery!" Tiny chides
As he hands me my cup of sorbet
And ambles over to the cash register
Where Bud is drumming his fingers on the counter

I stop at the toppings bar
Loading my cup with strawberries

The part of the treat
I might actually eat
Before going out to the front porch
That wraps around the store
Where everyone sits
In wrought-iron chairs
Around a glass chip mosaic table

Sniffles has followed me out
Wiggling his way between my feet
As I sit down next to Cody
I lean down and
Rub Sniffles around the ears
Catching the tip of his tail with the ends of my fingers
As he makes his way over to Asia

Asia scoops up Sniffles
Sets him on the table
"Asia! Why do you have to put him up here like that?" Micah
    complains.
"Don't be a baby. Everyone is holding their ice cream
    anyway," Asia says.

Which is lucky
Because just as she says it
Sniffles wrinkles his nose
Lets loose with a sneeze
That nearly knocks him off the table
"Poor little guy. Who ever heard of a dog with hay fever?"
    Asia croons
As she runs her hands up and down Sniffles's sides

"Perfect. Now there's a sneezing dog on the table," Micah
    groans.
"Such a drama queen," Asia sighs
Giving Sniffles one last scratch on his back.
He makes his way over to me
For more attention

I pull a napkin
From the dispenser in the middle of the table
Thinking I'll be funny
And pretend to wipe his nose

But I'm too slow
To catch the second sneeze that comes
Complete with a shower of doggie slobber
That sprays my sorbet and the table

Sniffles's tail goes into overdrive
He clamors into my lap
Rubbing his whiskery face against my chest
Cody is laughing
Micah and Kierra are too
As I push my away sorbet

If I wasn't so grateful
To this little dog
The fact that Asia isn't laughing
At all
Would bother me
More

BROKEN BALES

Dad loaded the hay before he left
Squaring the bales
On the bed of the truck
Making it easy for me
And Blue
Riding tall in the passenger seat

To find the perfect spot
On the crest of the hill
At the top of the pasture
Where I can put the truck into neutral
So Blue and I can run around
Hop on the bed
As the truck rolls forward

Slow enough for me to cut the twine
Kick the bales
Into the pasture
Where they break apart
For the cattle trailing along behind
First one bale
Then the next
Until they're gone
Save three

I jump over the side of the bed
Sliding back into the driver's seat
Catching a glimpse of Blue in the rearview mirror
Dashing back and forth

In the truck bed
Barking at the cattle
Reminding them that he'll be back
To head
To heel
To pen them
Next time need be

I swing the door shut
Pop the truck
Back into gear
Making my way toward
The horses
Already gathering at the gate
In front of the barn
Knowing that the bales with the sweetest hay
Have been stashed against the cab
Saved
Just for them

I count the horses down
Six
Five
Four
Coming up short
Just before
One

Scanning the fence line
For a break in the wire
I see something worse
Than an hour or two

Of fixing fence
The silhouette of a roan
Head down
In the shadow of a tree

Rocky
The one horse
The only horse
Neither Dad or I
Ride

Knowing we should
But not having the heart
To climb on this gelding
With the rose red mane
Who went off his feed
After my mom
Died

Dad said he would eat
Eventually
But I wasn't sure
Couldn't take watching
Another body
Whittled
Down to bones

So I filled buckets with bran mash
Cut up apples
Mixed them with molasses and cob grain
Put alfalfa cubes dusted with brown sugar

In a black rubber feeder
And sat in the glow of the harvest moon
With him
Night after night

As first I just sat
On the gate
With the bucket of feed
First one type
Then the next
In my lap
Running my fingertips
Over his muzzle
As the crickets strummed their legs
In a serenade

But Rocky wouldn't eat
Just stared
Past me
At the house
Wishing
Waiting for
Her
To come out

He didn't know
Couldn't understand
That she was gone
In a never-coming-back sort of way
How do you explain
That to a horse?

Maybe it was
Being locked into the silence
That comes with grief
But one night
I began to talk

Telling Rocky stories
About my mom
Before she got sick
Asking him questions

What it felt like
When she wrapped her arms around his neck
In a cowgirl hug
After they won Nationals
Her senior year

What she whispered to him
When she pressed her cheek against his
Before she swung into the saddle
And he carried her down the aisle
To marry
My dad

Had he been nervous
When my mom carried me
Nine days new
Out to the pasture
To meet him?

At first it was one ear
Twitching toward me

The other trained
On the house
Still waiting
Still wanting
To see her

But eventually
His head turned
His lips began to nibble
At the treats
In the bucket
In my hands

So that's what I did
Night after night
Talking
Sometimes even laughing
With Rocky
Remembering
Her

But now
His head is down
Hoof pawing the ground
Even from here
I can tell
This isn't
Good

TEMPERATURE, PULSE, RESPIRATION

Some say you should put a colicky horse in the trailer
Take them for a ride
Let them stomp
Hope the road bounces
The colic out

Others say keep them walking
Even let them lie down
But whatever you do
Make sure they don't
Roll

Torsion
Rupture
Impaction
Gallop over the top of my diagnostic list
As I fish the lead rope and halter
From behind the driver's seat
Kept there for
Emergencies

The halter goes on
Over Rocky's muzzle
Buckles
Behind his ears

I run my hand down his
Neck
Chest

Flanks
Dark with sweat
Nostrils flaring
With breaths
Coming too fast
Too shallow

Surgical versus medical
I wish I knew
How long
He's been
Like this

I press my ear to his side
Just below his ribs
Needing to hear
Gurgling
Grumbling
Hearing only
Silence

Forefingers slide down
Just below his jawbone
Counting the beats
Thrumming

Ten more
Then there should be
Within the space
Of a minute

Palm to his barrel
Each in and out
Equals one
Breath

Passing the magic number
Fifteen
Before the second hand
Makes it once
Around

Blue jumps off the bed
Knows I need his help
To get Rocky
    moving like his feet
    are mired in glue
To the barn

A step and then a stop
I give him the cue
Gentle, Blue
Setting off the nipping
At the fetlock joints
That gets Rocky moving

The other horses are interested now
Thinking about the grain
Not the first aid kit
I keep in the barn
As they fall in behind
Rocky

Who is moving
Moving slow

In the Tupperware box
Stashed under my saddle rack
Stocked with vet wrap
Betadine and gauze
There's Banamine too
In the dust-covered fridge

But I can't give that
Not yet
Dr. Katy will need to see Rocky first
Symptoms unmasked

TIME STOPS

A minute becomes
A millennium
After the call is placed
To the vet

Waiting
Watching
For her truck to appear
At the end of the road

As I pull and
Blue pushes
With gentle nips
To keep Rocky
Walking
Up and down the hard-packed path
Alongside
The barn

Ignoring the weight of the phone
In my back pocket
Reminding me of the second call
I haven't made
To Dad
At least not yet

He'll be worried
Imagining the worst

Of the 101 things
Rocky's colic could be

Assuming his cell could even pick up my call
As he drives across the state
Transporting cattle in his semi
To the sale yard
Where they'll burst out of the belly of the truck
Onto the ramps
Stopped cold
Blinded by the sun
Shocked still by the sight of the other cattle
Bellowing and charging
Up and down the maze of chutes and alleys
Leading into the sale ring

    Going once
    Going twice
    From hoof to rail
    Sold to the highest bidder

That's what I tell myself anyway
Words to cover up the fact
That part of me feels
This is my fault
Getting home
Later than usual
Feeding
Later than usual

Knowing that I switched dewormers
This month

Opting for a new brand
Guaranteed to wipe out
Ascarids to pin worms
Had it been too strong?

Not that it would matter
To a younger horse
But Rocky
Isn't young
Not anymore

The sickest part of all this
Is that underneath the push
And the pull of my conscience
        always eager to assign blame
I don't mind the walking

Each step I take
Negates the calories
I ingested
Today

Lighter
Leaner
Faster

My goal
Is always
There

BLUE YIPS

Yanks me from my reverie
He dashes up the drive
Canine chauffeur
For Dr. Katy
As she pulls her truck up to the barn
Pulls on her Dickies
As she steps out

"Well, this guy is looking good," she says as she leans down
    and scratches Blue around the ears. "He's not who I'm here
    for though, is he? Let's get Rocky into the stocks."
Rocky groans as I tug his lead
Coaxing him into the barn
Through the palpation stocks
Stopping him with the gate
That closes across his chest

Dr. Katy is close behind
Swinging the back gate closed
As she moves around to his side
Stethoscope in hand
"How long has he been like this?" she asks.
I'm not sure exactly. I called you right when I found him.
She nods her head
As she puts in the earpiece
Listens

I take my position
Alongside Rocky

Lead rope in hand
Making sure he stays up
As Dr. Katy listens to his GI tract
Before checking
    temperature
        pulse
            respiration
                capillary refill

Finally moving toward the back of the chute
For the rectal examination
"Let's see if we can do this without a twitch."

I slide to the front of the chute
Kneading Rocky's ears
It's going to be all right, I whisper
Hoping it will
Not knowing if I have the heart
To twirl the loop of rope at the end of the twitch
Around his whiskery nose

Rocky's head jerks up
He sways
Stomps the rubber mat beneath his hooves
As Dr. Katy's hand slides in

Rocky stomps again
Hard
My cue to grab the skin
On the right side of his neck
Hard

My hand a fist
Of skin and hair
Creating a diversion
From Dr. Katy
An endorphin rush for him
My fingers start to cramp
But I can't let go
Not until Dr. Katy is done

I want to ask
What she is finding
    knowing which words
      I don't want to hear
But Dr. Katy isn't one to talk
Not during an exam

Dr. Katy pulls her arm out
Glove off
Gives me a nod
My cue to lead Rocky from the stocks
To follow her outside

Where she grabs a metal bucket
Fills it with water
From her truck
Before grabbing tubing
          pump
     oil

Dr. Katy drapes the tubing around her neck
Drops a dollop of lube

On her hand
Runs it along the tube

The cotton lead is rough against my palm
Soaked wet with rain
Dried hard by the sun
More than a time or two
I run my hand up to the clip
At the base of the halter
Gentle pressure
A tug not a pull
As I tease his neck round

Rocky breaks at the poll
Creating a smoother path for the tube
Dr. Katy is ready to slide
Up his nasal passage
Down his throat

Her right hand slides over the top of his muzzle
Fingers hook
Around to his nostril
Holding his head still
Still as can be expected
When a tube is being run down a horse's esophagus

Dr. Katy takes the end of the tube in her mouth and blows
Rocky swallows
I can see the tube moving down
His throat
As she feeds it though his esophagus
Into his stomach

You can smell when it gets there
The gas from his stomach
    That can't push food out
    Not like ours can anyway
    Throwing up
    When something makes us sick
Smells like ingesta
Alfalfa and bile

Dr. Katy reaches down
Takes the metal pump
From the bucket
Primes one
    Two
Three
Moving the water through first
As she lavages his stomach
With one bucket
Then two

The mineral oil comes next
Rocky stands through it all
Seeming to know
That this is what it will take
To make him better
Again

Finally, the pump comes off
The tube comes out
Dr. Katy coils it up
Places it in the bucket
Pulls a syringe out of her back pocket

Places her thumb
In the jugular furrow

Occlusion
The vein bulges
The needle slides in
Blood flushes the Banamine red as Dr. Katy pulls the plunger
  back
Before pushing the medicine in
Holding off the site
Before a bubble of blood blooms
Where she pulls the needle out

"Now, we wait and see," she says.
As if it's as simple as that

DON'T BE A HERO

It was midnight
Before I pulled my phone
From my pocket
Dad was already on his way home

"You should have called," he said.
Like I knew
He would

I should have.
I say
Throwing in an excuse
About how fast it had all gone
Finding Rocky
Calling
Waiting for
Helping the vet

Not mentioning
The hours
Between then
And now
When it has just been
Rocky
Blue
And me

Walking
Waiting

For Rocky's GI tract
To relax
Enough for the manure and gas
That had been tying him up
To pass

"But he's going to be okay?" Dad asks.
I lean into Rocky
Pressing my forehead
To his

Rocky's breath is warm
Against my chest
The night air cool
Around my shoulders
He is.

"You need to call me when things like this happen," Dad says.
"Pick up the phone and I'll be there. Don't be a hero."

I know. I'm sorry, Dad.
His name, Dad,
Catches on a tear
Tears the sentence
In half

"Hey, Sweetie. I'm sorry. I didn't mean—"
I know, Dad. It's not you. I'm just tired.
"Of course you are. I want you to put that horse up and get
    yourself to bed. I'll be home soon, okay?"
The radio station jumps from station to station in the background
    It's something he does when he's trying to stay awake

Turns the music up
The air conditioner on

I worry about him driving
This late at night
Okay. I love you, Dad.
"I love you too."

Dad hangs up
But I keep the phone
Pressed to my ear
And say it again
I'm sorry, Dad.

I lean into Rocky's chest
Slide down his front legs
Blue comes
To sit on my boots
His nub of a tail wagging
As he smiles up at me

Even with this horse
Who carries a part of my mom
This dog
Who carries a part of my heart
Pressed into me

I can't turn them off
These tears
Because I know
What a hero
Doesn't do

A hero doesn't tally the calories
She's walking off
As her mom's horse
Lathers with pain

Who does that?

And when did that person
Become
Me

THAT IS THE QUESTION

Today has been hard
Running on almost no sleep
After being up with Rocky

Asia knows that
Which is why
I can't believe she's asking me
Now
Fifth block
Fifteen minutes before the final bell
"So you can't stay?"
She is my ride home
Or was supposed to be

Snide words serpentine
On the back of my tongue
Because why wouldn't I
Want to sit in front of a computer screen
Between Asia
And Kierra
    "She's going to show us the website she made for their
        team last year and explain how she put it together.
        It won't take long," Asia says. "Once I see it I'll have a
        better idea which pictures to include on ours."
We're supposed to be creating found poems
Which usually requires reading
And writing
Asia isn't even pretending
To do either

Her camera is in her lap
Beneath her desk
As she scans pictures
So much more interesting
Than *Hamlet*

"Like this one."
She passes me the camera
On the screen is a picture
Of Micah
His rope looped round
As his horse explodes out of the box
Chasing the black-and-white blur of a steer
Across the arena

Will it be clear enough for the website?
Asia takes the camera back
Rubs her thumb across the screen
"Probably not. See? That's why I need you!"

I sigh
Wishing I could take it back as soon as I do
Trauma drama isn't me
At least
It didn't used
To be

It's not like I can't get a ride home from Cody
If I choose not to stay
But still
I wish you would have said something earlier.

Asia puts her camera back in its case
"I know. I'm sorry. Things have just been so crazy today, I forgot."
Which actually makes sense
Midmorning pep assembly coupled with a precalc exam
Equals an understandable excuse
But still

I shouldn't. I have to take care of some things this afternoon.
It's my vague excuse
That clues her in
"It's because it's her, isn't it?"
No. I just have things to do.
Asia raises an eyebrow
"Okay."

Assuming I'll stay late
Acting put out if I don't
The words on the page of my textbook pitch and roll
I pin them down with my eyes
Because I am not angry
　　jealous
　　　　betrayed

"Seriously, Rae. We aren't going to be that long."
Asia shoves her camera into her backpack
"Please? You know I'll need your opinion."

Which is true
Without it
Asia will hover
Between the maybes
Of making a decision

I glance at the clock
Above the door
Two minutes to go
A verdict is due
Sure, I say.
Like it's nothing
    Fingertips find my vertebrae
    Five-four-three-two-one
Hoping that it is

CLUTTERED

I picture someone coming in
Looking at us from the back
The three of us
All in a row
Staring at Kierra's computer screen

If someone saw us like this
Three girls
They'd never guess that one
Feels odd girl
Out

That one is me
Acting normal
Feeling off
Creeping around the hole
I have created
Between Kierra and I
Because I just can't
Forgive and forget

"I'm not trying to be mean, but seriously, look at their page,"
    Kierra's saying.
Clicking on the drop-down menu of a what-not-to-do page
"It's not horrible," Kierra says. "Just—"
"Cluttered," Asia finishes.
"Exactly."

And confused
I want to add
Realizing it's me
Not the website
That's a pick-up-sticks
Mess

"Now look at ours,"
Ever-so-humble Kierra says.
"I love it," Asia says.
I want to wipe away
The adoration
That drips
Off her words
"I had a lot of help," Kierra says.

"What do you think, Raesha?" Asia turns toward Kierra. "She
   took computer applications last year. Got an A."
This last part was for Kierra
An explanation
As to why my opinion matters
It's really clean. Professional.

Generous words
From a generous heart
Because that's what I am
A generous girl

I get up from my chair
Step away
Pretending to check my phone
As the two of them chat

Head to head
About this soon-to-be project
That really doesn't
Include
Me

DELIVERY

"I told you they'd be the only ones here," Cody says
As he and Micah walk through the door
With a pizza and sodas
"He was worried there'd be a bunch of other people working
    and—" Cody begins.
Asia spins around
Springs out of her chair
"And you wouldn't have brought enough for everyone, right?"
She says as she lays a kiss on Micah's cheek
"My sweet guy."

Cody bats his eyes
Clutches his hands
To his heart
"You're such a love, Micah."
Cody drapes his arms around my shoulders
Pulls me close in a hug
Sets a can of Coke
Diet
In front of me
"How much have you missed me?"

Tons.
"Hey, Kierra," Cody says
Leaning in to look at the website on her computer screen
"Nice! You designed this?"
Kierra clicks through the drop-down menu
For Cody and Micah now

So in love with these pictures
That I don't need to see

I stand back
Still odd girl out
Until Cody peels off
Remembers the pizza
That's beginning to get cold

He doesn't even ask
Just hands them out
Paper plates stacked high
Enough pizza for a couple of slices each

He hands me mine
Not noticing the way
I flinch at the smell

Pepperoni
"Your favorite," he says.
I guess it used to be
Knowing he got it
For me

A kiss on the cheek, and he slides
Back to the computers
To look at the pictures
I opt
Not to see

Preferring to stare
At this plate in my hands
Than the backs
Of my friends

A FEW ALTERATIONS

Since I haven't eaten all day
    aside from the coffee
    (ten calories a cup)
    that has kept me awake
I can afford this
I tell myself
Pizza
Just one slice
With a few alterations

First the pepperoni
It has to go
Stacked in a tower
On the edge
Of the plate

I grab a wad of napkins
From beside the box
Lay one across a slice
A sponge
Soaking up the grease
Pooled on top
Of the cheese

First one napkin
Then two
The cheese sticks to the third
Which is fine
Because I don't need that

Loaded
With
Fat

"What are you doing, weirdo?" Cody asks.
Guilty as charged
I scrunch up the napkins
Cringe as the oil leaks
Coats my hand
Nothing.

"You mutilated that thing."
He gestures at my slice
A triangle of crust and sauce
I—
Asia glares
Less than impressed
By what she thinks
I'm doing

I've been sick to my stomach a lot lately. I think it might be cheese.
"What?" Cody says.
I just—
    I mean—
        I might be allergic. Lactose intolerant. So I'm not doing
        cheese right now.

Asia is still staring
Not buying my speech at all

Cody looks at Micah
Searching for some help

Micah shrugs
Because who doesn't eat
Cheese?

"Whatever," Cody says.
Topic closed
Loads up another plate
Hands it to Kierra
"You aren't going to maim your slice, are you?" Cody asks.

Kierra laughs
"No, I love to eat. Especially pizza."
"That's what I'm talking about," Cody grins.
"Let me see your pictures, Asia," Micah says.
Entirely over the pizza talk

And now it's them
Four in a row
Backs to me
Studying Asia's photos

"We'll have to bring it up in the meeting tomorrow," Micah
    says.
So in love
With this idea
And not just because Asia is excited
Even though
That helps

"Or we could wait until we get the website up and running,"
    Kierra suggests.
"Even better!" Asia agrees. "A dramatic unveiling!"

Because she has always been one
For flair

Not that I care
Still standing
Off to the side
Minus five
No one's looking
I wrap my pizza in a napkin
Fold my plate in half
Into the trash
Gone
Minus five

No one noticed
And what
If they did?

IMPROMPTU MEETING

For me anyway
Because I forgot about it
Entirely
I seem to do that a lot lately
Forget things
I normally wouldn't

Which Asia is quick to point out
"You seriously don't remember? We talked about it yesterday
　　in the computer lab."
No, I—
"Whatever. Let's go," Asia says.
All rush
No patience
Noting my empty hands
"Go grab your lunch and meet me there."

Leaving me standing in the hall
Wondering what I should do
About the lunch
I didn't bring
As she links up with Micah
Halfway down the hall
Heading toward Mr. Retsom's room

A paper that needed doing
Extensive research
Library time required
Was supposed to have been my excuse

Today
But I know that won't fly

The meeting will be short
All listening
Maybe a vote
And then
We'll be done
I think

Maybe I can get away
With an empty desk
Even though everyone else
Will be eating
I'll get something afterward
At least that's what I'll say

FASHIONABLY LATE

I slip into Mr. Retsom's room
The meeting already underway
Insurance that no one will be able to ask
Where my lunch
Is

Cody saved me a desk
Next to his
Listening to Asia and Kierra
Explaining
What I'm assuming
Is going to be our fund-raiser this year

"Get ready to sell some tickets," Cody whispers,
Tipping his head in the direction of the dry-erase board
"Tri-tip Beef Dinner!"
Is written in red and blue bubble letters
Awesome.
I mouth

Cody holds up half of the sandwich he's eating
It's tuna
I can smell it
"Where's your lunch?"
Asia hears him this time
Gives him the eye

"Stop talking to me, Raesha! I'm trying to listen."
Only this time his voice is a few decibels louder

He's so funny
Or at least
That's what he thinks

Sliding the half of his sandwich he hasn't touched yet
Onto my desk
As he stares straight ahead
Hyperfocused
Ultrainterested in
What Asia is saying

It's such a simple
Kind
Gesture
But tuna
Specifically, the mayonnaise
Will knock me three steps back
From my goal

The tomato
Lettuce
They will work
So I pick at those
Pulling them from between the slices of bread
Wishing I had a napkin
To wipe them off

"I'm thinking we'll hold the dinner at the clubhouse," Asia says
Turning to Kierra to further describe the location
"It's the big building behind the fairgrounds. Huge kitchen.
    Meeting hall. Just up from the creek."

"We could do it outside if the weather is nice," Cody suggests.
I like this idea even better
Preferring to think about a fund-raiser
Rather than Cody's sandwich
We could put up patio lights.
"Decorate the gazebo. Do linen tablecloths like they do for
    wedding receptions," Asia continues.
"It sounds perfect," Kierra says.

How grateful am I
To receive this pronouncement from her
Ordaining the location
That she has never even seen
Not up close anyway
Appropriate

Asia grabs a dry-erase marker
That she hands to me
My cue to
Start the to-do list
She is creating aloud
That starts with the tickets
That will need to be printed and sold

It's impossible not to notice
Cody's eyes slide
From the front of the room
To my desk
Left vacant
And the sandwich
I pretend to have forgotten

NEVER EVER

Mr. Kraftner clears his throat as he sits back down at his desk
His hand absently searching for the cup of coffee
Almost buried in the stacks of papers
He's grading

Cody glances at Mr. Kraftner as he pulls a Kit Kat from his
    backpack
"We've got to get this done. I can't have homework."
He doesn't have to say it
Because I know
Rodeo team practice
I've got it too

Cody unwraps the candy bar and breaks it
Half for him
Half for me
I set the Kit Kat on my desk
Where it makes a perfect pencil holder
I lay one in the groove between the wafers
I'm so innovative
Maybe I should patent this

Cody breaks his bars in half and slides them into his mouth
"Don't you want it?"
Sure. Only not right now.
Or ever
It's not that I can't eat the candy bar
Because I could
If I wanted to

I just know
How the calories will seep through my body
Accumulate on my thighs
    my hips
        my stomach
            my—

"But Kit Kats are your favorite," he says.
I just don't want to eat it this second. Is that all right?
The harsh syllables ricochet
Cody pulls his legs out of the aisle
Sits up straight

He picks up his ball cap from the corner of his desk
Kneads the bill in his hands
"I guess. It just seems like you never—"
Never what?
"I don't know." Cody stares at his ball cap. "Never mind."

Even with the sun streaming in through the windows
I'm cold
I slide my hands under my legs
One of my knuckles pops
As I roll my weight
Back and forth
Pressing the bones of my hands
Against my chair
It hurts

Cody looks at my arms
Where goose bumps have my hairs standing at attention
"Are you cold? Here."

Cody pulls his sweatshirt over his head and hands it to me
I slide my arms into the sleeves
It is soft
Still warm
I stare at my textbook
Unopened
On my desk

Cody shoves the last piece of his candy bar in his mouth
He crunches it a few times and moves his lips around like a cow
"Do I have something in my teeth?"
Cody grins big
Showing off the chocolate chunks
Pressed into his teeth

Laughter bubbles up from my middle
Washing away my stress
Cody's smiling
Because I'm smiling
At his grade-school joke

My pencil comes off my makeshift pencil holder
It smells like chocolate now
Cody's writing already
So I'd better catch up
I open my textbook
But my thoughts are stuck on the
You never

Never what?
Never smile
Never laugh

Never eat
Never ever?

I eat
If I had a problem
Which I don't
I'd never eat
I'm just fastidious
About what I put in my mouth

"What'd you get for number six?" Cody asks.
What? I look down at my notebook.
My pencil stopped moving somewhere between my name and
    the first problem
Cody looks at my page
At the clock on the wall above the door
At me
At the Kit Kat still on my desk

"Come on, Raesha. You haven't even started."
Never do my part
Can't finish what you don't start
Sorry. Give me a minute and I'll catch up.
Cody nods

I try to push numbers through the equation
Everything's about numbers
About making them fit
Numbers that I can't slide into this equation
No matter how hard I try

I must be stupid
Because I can't make them work
All these numbers in my head are making me crazy
Maybe I am crazy

The bell rings
We're done
Books close
Cody's got homework
I've got more

More time
With more numbers
That I've got to make
Fit

FOREVER INDEBTED

Asia races up from behind
Catches me around the shoulders
In a hug
Half tackle
Nearly knocking me down
As I step out of class
And into the hallway

"She's getting a truck donated! A truck!"
I don't know what she's talking about
All I feel is annoyed
As my graph paper slips out of my binder
And fans
Across the floor

Cody is right behind me
Kneeling down
To gather my papers
While I extricate myself from Asia's
Half nelson hug

Asia, stop! What are you even talking about?
"Kierra's dad is going to donate a truck!"
To—
"To us!"

Cody stands
Hands me the haystack of paper
"Are you serious? A new truck?"

"No, a junker," Asia teases. Too excited to be truly frustrated.
    "Yes! A new truck!"
I'm not getting it
For the team?
"Yes!"

Asia gives up on us
Cody
The diesel engine connoisseur turned skeptic
And me
Just out of the loop
Neither showing nearly enough enthusiasm
Turning instead to Micah
Walking down the hall toward us

"Micah! You don't have to ask for donations for the auction
    anymore!"
I can tell by his smile that Micah doesn't even care why
"Kierra's dad is donating a truck! A new truck!"
Micah looks at Cody and me
The arch in his eyebrow
Shows he's wondering
If this is a joke
"How did that happen?" he asks.
"Her dad owns a dealership in Nebraska. It will be a huge tax
    write-off for him."

I can't help wondering when Kierra's dad
Suddenly appeared
What with her living with her grandma

And him
Not even in
The same state

"So instead of candy bars and car washes—" Cody begins.
"Or a silent auction—" Micah chimes in.
"We're going to sell raffle tickets for a truck!"
"Are we even going to have a dinner then?" I ask.
Wondering who can do that
Give away
A truck

"Yes. Instead of a silent auction, we'll announce the winner at
   the dinner," Asia says.
"I guess you'll have to return all those items you've gotten
   donated, Micah," Cody says.
"I would have gotten more if I'd had any help," he says.
Cody traces the path of an imaginary tear down his cheek
"Did you even get any?" Asia asks.
"No, but—"
"Whatever. It doesn't matter!" Asia says. "I have to go find Mr.
   Bradford. Kierra and I are meeting up with him to conference
   call her dad in about five minutes. We have to figure out how
   to do all the paperwork for such a huge donation!"

Asia throws in a few skips and a twirl
As she disappears into the after-school throng
Leaving me
Without a ride home

"Do you care if we drop off Micah first?" Cody asks.
"I've got little-sister babysitting duty," Micah explains.
Since I'll be occupying the middle of the bench seat
In Cody's truck
Sure. I don't mind, I say,
And fall into step with Cody and Micah

"I hope it's a nice truck," Cody says.
"If it's new it doesn't matter."
"True. Even if it's a base model—"

I know this is only the beginning
Of the truck talk
That won't end
Until we drop Micah off

Not that I mind
It just would have been nice—
I mean
I could have helped
Figure out the paperwork
If Asia
Had asked

ALMOST

Look at our legs
Our arms
Pushing cotton shirtsleeves to our shoulders
Hiking up our shorts
To show off our suntans

At least that's what we called them
Loving the way the dust
Coated us brown
After it settled on our skin
Pounded out of the earth by our horses' hooves
Loping after the cattle we knew better than to chase
But did

Asia always gave up first
Went in easier
For a bath to wash off her tan
My mom let it slide
Holding back the laughter
Gathering behind her lips
Shut tight in a smile
Enchanted by my grade-school vanity
Letting me slip between my sheets
Swooned into sleep by the smell
The feel
Of the dust and the sky against my skin

Maybe that's what fills me up
The dust and the sky

Wrapping around my shoulders
Even after the day I've had
As I walk around the arena
Fancy right behind
Long way back to the trailer
Fancy's breath on the back of my hand
Coming softer now
Walking the sweat that darkened her neck and chest
Dripped from beneath her saddle pad
Dry

Watching Asia make her last run
Yelling her luck
As she and Scuba trace the cloverleaf round
Knowing before the electric eye blinks
That it's hers
Best time of the night

I need to find Cody
But for now
I want to savor this
Moment
When everything feels so right
I can almost believe
I'm enough
Just as I
Am

A MOMENT TOO LONG

When people ask me what my favorite color is
I say green
Because I don't know what to call it
This color the sky turns
When the sun and moon meet
One setting
The other rising
Winking at each other through the indigo touched with gold

It only lasts a moment
The sky looking this way
I know I should go
Keep walking
To the other end of the arena
Where Cody's waiting

But it will only be a moment
So I climb onto the fence
Green metal panels hinge-pinned together
Forming the catacomb of pens off to the side of the arena

To inhale the sky
This color
Before it's swallowed by the black
Dragged in by the moon
I am at peace

I can see him from here
In the space between the trucks and trailers

With eight
Maybe nine
Other ropers
Winding and tossing loops
At the hay bale steer

So busy laughing at their ropes
Coming to rest around
Bouncing off
The bovine mannequin's plastic head
They don't notice it
The color of the sky

It's sad
Them not noticing
I wonder if I should show Cody
Come up behind him
Wrap my arms around his waist
Lift his eyes to the sky with the words I breathe into his ear
I should show him
Before it's too late
Before the magic is gone

That suddenly doesn't matter
Because all I can see is Kierra
Come out from behind his truck
Climb onto the side of the bed
To sit with her legs dangling
Heels hooked on the wheel well
Of Cody's truck

She's not looking at the sky
Or the hay bale steer
Head anatomically correct
Except for the plastic smile
Just at Cody
Standing with his back to her
Close enough for her to swipe his ball cap
Off his head

He spins on his heels
Grabbing at the hat
She's flagging through the air
Laughing so wild
So hard
That she falls
Off the edge of the bed
Into
Onto
Him

Not letting go
Of his shoulders
Neither of them pushing out of the leaning
That's pressing them together
So close he notices a smudge
An eyelash
On her cheek
Wiping it off with his thumb

The ocean filling my ears
Roars
With waves

The water
Rushing in so fast it's hard to see
To understand
Why
He didn't push away
Out of the arms around his shoulders
Cody
My Cody

Who I suddenly don't know

IF I WERE

If I was the kind of girlfriend to get angry
Or jealous
This would bother me
But since I'm not
It doesn't

Because technically it's Mrs. Morrison
Who sent them to the library together
Paired for a health project
That doesn't really matter
Even if he does it with her
Instead of with me

Because it's Mrs. Morrison's idea that they be a pair
Mrs. Morrison who sent them off to the library to pick up the
    books
For their project
That doesn't include me
        not that I care
        because I'm not the kind of girlfriend who gets jealous
        wastes energy getting mad over decisions that have
        nothing to do with me
Even after what I saw
Last
Night

But the thing is
Mrs. Morrison sent me to the office after they left
To pick up copies

Technically I could go
Should go
Have gone directly to the office
Rather than through the hallway
That bisects our school
Library on one side
Computer lab on the other
But I don't

Which is why I'm here now
In the doorway of the library
Where Cody and Kierra sit
At a round table in the middle of the library
With a book spread open between them
    when they could each be using their own
Sitting side by side, talking and laughing
    when they should be sitting across from each other

Kierra looks over her shoulder
Stalker
    Stalker
Caught
Acknowledges me with a smile
As she drapes her arm
Around the back
Of Cody's chair

Before she turns away
From me
Sliding her attention across the table
Back to him
Cody

My Cody
Laughing and talking
With her

Not even seeing me
Standing
Here

I KNOW WHAT I SAW

I didn't say anything
But as irrational as I know this is
I feel like he should know
Sense
That I saw them

More specifically
Saw Kierra
With her arm
Around him

I know I'm being crazy
Because if I would have asked Cody
Would have mentioned that I saw them
First, last night
And then today
Sitting like that
If I could have heard that the laughing and the library were
    nothing
That he hadn't even noticed her arm
Around the back of his chair
Then I would probably be
All right

But the thing is
I don't trust myself
To bring it up
Because lately
Jagged words

Fly
Out of my mouth
Before I can stop
Them

Which is why I'm sitting here
At the lunch table
Next to him
Staring at the brown paper bag
Holding a sandwich
I'm not going to eat

Leaner
Lighter
Faster
Minus five

"Does your dad still need my help tonight, Rae?" Cody asks
Reminding me that they were going to fix something
On the engine of the tractor
That broke down
With a round bale balanced on the implement
Halfway to the feeder
The other night
I'm guessing so. The tractor's still out in the middle of the pasture.

"What are you doing to it?" Micah asks.
Cody pops his milk carton open
As he launches into a conversation
About diesel engines
That I wish I cared
About

Reassuring myself that he will be
At my house
Not hers
Tonight
Working with my dad

I scan the cafeteria for Asia
Wanting her here
Even though I know she'll notice
My lunch
Still in the sack

I just want to run it by her
Before I bring it up with him
The arm
Around him
The chair?
Not to mention
The smile

But I'm not seeing her
Wondering where Asia could be
Micah—
Hearing how rude I am
As I interrupt
Do you know where—

Cody elbows me
Accidentally
As he lifts his hand
    returns her wave from across the cafeteria

Which smells like the tomato sauce
That should have gone on the spaghetti
Until it burned hard
Which is why everyone has crammed into the line
Where she is standing
Waiting for the pizza they are serving instead
She waves

I elbow Cody back
On purpose
On accident?
As I slam away from the lunch table

Leaving Cody openmouthed
His eyes asking why
I'm being so crazy
Again

JUST TELL HIM

Asia's family can't possibly eat at this table
Clean laundry is stacked into towers
That never seem to end
Asia pushes a pile of shirts to the side
Sets down her cup of cocoa
"It's not a big deal. Not unless you make it into one. Just tell
    him you're sorry. Call him."

This comes after
Me crying
Her listening
About how angry I'd gotten in the cafeteria
Wondering if Cody could ever
Forgive me
For forgetting I'm not the kind of girlfriend to get angry or
    jealous
Asia promising he would

Because that's what best friends do
Even when they don't really
Know
Can't help but
Feel
Confused about it all

We both know that Cody
The guy who found a hundred-dollar bill
On the floor
Of the movie theater

And turned it in to the manager
Last month
Doesn't have it in him
To cheat
On me

Blue and Cow sit on either side of me
Canine bookends
Resting their chins on my legs
Stepping away to make room for Alexi
Back from feeding
    her horse—
    her goats—
    and her seven lop-eared rabbits
Monday through Sunday
    one named for each day of the week
To crawl into my lap
Still wearing her coveralls and black rubber barn boots
Plucking a dryer sheet out of the stack of laundry to wipe away
   my tears
Suggesting that cookies always made her feel better
Especially the ones with M&M's in them
"Blow," she'd instructed.
Holding the dryer sheet to my nose
Not understanding why anyone would be embarrassed about
   being sad
Just glad that Asia and I were laughing again

So we followed Alexi's lead
Singing "Happy Birthday to You" three times while soaping
   our hands
Just like her teacher had taught her

Because "germs are not our friends!" Alexi proclaimed.
Leading us from the bathroom
Back into the kitchen
Where her barn boots left dusty prints edged with alfalfa on the
    linoleum

First their mom
Then their dad
In from work
In from chores
Shaking their heads and laughing at the three of us
Alexi sitting on the counter
Separating the green M&M's
Because they were special
The best
And had to be eaten before the rest went in the cookie dough
Asia and I sifting and mixing and measuring
With the precision of preschoolers
Enlisting Blue and Cow as our official taste testers

Alexi rolled a lump of dough
Into a ball
Flattened it with her palm before
Giving it two eyes
        a nose
            an M&M mouth
Cooking it until the edges started to brown
"For you," she said.
When it came out of the oven
Which meant I couldn't say no

Not with Asia watching me
So I took one bite
Then two
>   Leaner
>   Lighter
>   Faster
Knowing I shouldn't
But Asia's shoulders relaxed
With each bite I took
Which made it worth it

Let me believe
That if I can do this
Then maybe anything
Even forgiveness
Is possible

WHAT I DIDN'T SEE

That good feeling from last night is still hanging around my
    shoulders
It followed me out the door from Asia's house
All through today
Fills me with confidence as I pick the plate of cookies wrapped
    in foil
Off the seat of Asia's truck
Where I'd left them until I saw it pull in
Cody's rusted-out, dented-in orange truck and horse trailer
Parked on the other side of the arena

Knowing that on Saturdays the team ropers practice right after
    the barrel racers
Sure that Cody and Micah are pushing the steers in from the
    pasture
And into the pens
Where they'll funnel through one at a time
Dashing and skipping away from the cowboy's loops flying
    through the air

Sure that Cody was there watching just a few minutes earlier
When Fancy and I set the pace
Raised the bar
With our time
Best so far this season
Certainly earning her the coffee-can scoop of molasses sweet
    grain she's munching
Standing in the grass next to the trailer

Where I leave her
Setting off to find Cody

Looking to the pasture I see Asia on Scuba with Micah running
    alongside
Chasing behind the steers
Their hollering and slapping
Mixing with the rumbling of the hooves
Muted by the dust
Small beneath the sky stretching empty and blue

I see the red of the ball cap
With the frayed bill kneaded round
Bobbing on the other side of the green metal panels
Knowing before I see him
That he'll be fidgeting around at the gate
Ready to clang it shut behind the train
        of black
        white
        red
        rangy brindled hides

Knowing before I see him
That his white cotton roping gloves will be dangling out of his
    back pocket
That his breath will smell like the cinnamon gum he cracks
    when he rides
And that inside his boots, he'll be wearing his lucky socks
        red
        same as the color of his hat

Same as the color I see
When I turn the corner and see
Her
In his hat
Working the gate
With him leaning
On the panels beside
Her

Leaving me seeing only the red
Filling up my mouth
Drowning
Dropping that good feeling that was hanging around my
    shoulders
Into the dirt
With the cookies
And the trust

TEDDY BEAR BUDDY

Carpet squares and finger painting
Picture books and graham crackers
All I'd have to give up would be my lunch period
Fifty-eight minutes of wondering where to set
My tray
My words
Myself
Next to
Across from
The space I've created
Behind walls of assumption
Bricks mortared with suspicion
Unfounded
Between Cody and me

Under the guise of altruism, I flee
Across the parking lot into the building where the classrooms
Are decorated with dancing numbers
Where words are formed with letters shaped like animals
And being in high school makes me an adult
In the eyes of the students
Who haven't grown into the honor roll yet
Their progress charted with gold stars
By teachers wearing clogs and yarn sweaters with matching
    turtlenecks

Mrs. George
Smelling like lavender in her sturdy shoes and cardigan
Secretary and nurse all in one

Hugs me over the counter in the principal's office
Asking how it is
    with me
    my dad
    that lovely girl Asia—always tighter than two peas in a
        pod, we were
Pinning to my shirt a tag shaped like a teddy bear
With the words "Reading Buddy"
Printed across the bear's tummy in bubbly letters

"So sweet of you to give up your lunch hour," she says.
Directs me down the hall
Papered with pictures
Watercolor over crayon
Scenes of spring with rainbows
And clouds shaped like cotton balls

Into room two
Where Miss Dixon
    Who'd parted my hair and combed it smooth
    Weaving it into braids she'd tied with plaid ribbons
    While the rest of the class was streaming through the door
    Swinging lunch boxes and book bags
    Knowing that the hands chapped dry by the sun and the
        wind
That could wrestle a steer
And hug his little girl into a smile
Got tied up and confused with a brush and barrettes
Sat on the rug
Beneath the dancing numbers
Singing about spring and rainbows and clouds shaped like
    cotton balls

To eighteen kindergartners
Smaller than I could have ever been

Introducing me like a celebrity to my audience on the floor
Beckoning to a little girl sitting apart from the circle
The only one whose name I don't know
The only one not smiling
The only one interested in her shoes

Miss Dixon hands me a stack of books and expectations
For this little girl
So interested in her shoes
Who follows me to a corner
Where we sit on bean bags the color of lima beans
And read about dinosaurs on skateboards and penguins on skis
That aren't nearly as interesting as her shoes

Somewhere between the dinosaurs and the penguins
I notice that her braids
Streaked with sun
Are tied with plaid ribbons

Suddenly I want that dinosaur to make her smile
More than anything
For those penguins to make her look up from her shoes
And her socks
One yellow and one pink
The colors of spring

But they don't
So I leave the books and expectations on Miss Dixon's desk
With a promise

Not sure if she heard
Or cared
So interested in her shoes
My teddy bear buddy
That I'd be back

THAT KIND OF FRIEND

We've never fought
Not ever
Even now we're aren't really fighting
Mostly because I won't
I'm not the kind of friend
Who gets mad and yells
Over things that don't mean anything
Or everything

Sitting on the couch with our legs tucked under us tight
The cushion in the middle
Where our feet would usually tangle
Occupied by Asia's white patched cat
With extra toes who drools when she sleeps
Who usually never gets to lie on the furniture
Until now
Holding the space between me and Asia

Alexi and her cousin Anna Jay
Lie on the floor
Side by side
In their construction paper headbands with rabbit ears
Colored pink and white
Dressed for their sleepover
In matching yellow pajamas with ducks
Somersaulting across the pants
Slumber party twins
Filling in the charts in their 4-H notebooks with felt-tip pens
Following the growth

Pound by pound
Of their rabbits
Growing up strong for the fair

Leaving the living room silent and stiff
When they skip off
To a night of
Sleeping bag stories
Flashlight wars
Night-light giggles

Asia's dad pads into the living room in his wool socks and
    sweats
Hands us mugs of hot cocoa with cookie lids
Gingerbread chocolate chunk
Absorbing the steam and the heat from the cocoa
Leaving the middles gooey

If he notices the cat
Sprawled on the cushion
Absorbing the space
Made by me
Not being mad
At Asia
Not understanding why
The red is still filling up my eyes and mouth
Making it impossible for me to swallow and bow back
Into the four
That's now only three
He doesn't say anything except
"Good night."
As he picks up one of the coffee table magazines

Filled with articles on raising cattle
Plumped slow on hay and grass
Special-ordered by grocery stores called co-ops
Where customers carry their purchases home in fabric bags
With pictures of the world and evergreen trees on the front
Willing to pay more for meat grown
Organic
Clean

Leaving me and Asia staring over our mugs at each another
Since I'm not the kind of friend who gets mad and yells
Over things that don't mean
Anything
Or everything
I fill up the space talking about my teddy bear buddy
And how much the dinosaurs on skateboards mean to her
Not mentioning how she stares at her shoes
Or the plaid ribbons in her hair parted smooth and straight

"It's been almost a week," Asia interrupts.
Angry about my teddy bear buddy
About me
Leaving her to sit across the lunch table from Cody
To laugh too hard
Talk too much
To make up for the fact that there are three instead of four

"You don't have to do that, you know. Because I don't care
  about you not eating," she says.

I didn't even realize
I'd been poking the cookie

Piece by piece
Into my mug
With my thumb

Because the not being mad
Or worried
About anything
Everything
Is filling my heart
Leaking into my stomach
Leaving it too full
For the chocolate and the gingerbread
Falling into the mug
Floating
Breaking apart
Sinking

JUST CONFUSED

My legs are stuck to the seat of the truck
Not really
But they might as well be

Asia's already out of the cab with the truck box popped open
Fishing around for her backpack until her arm gets distracted
When she sees Cody and Micah pull into the parking lot
And waves

There's an empty spot next to us
I know that's where he's heading
Cody, pulling his rusted-out, dented-in orange truck
Through the grid of rigs
Strung through with people

Cody's truck rolls closer
My legs are still stuck
But they shouldn't be
Because this really isn't a big deal

Asia said he isn't mad
Just confused
I keep repeating that to myself
Isn't mad—Isn't mad
As he pulls in

It doesn't matter that I don't get out of the truck
Because Cody comes over and opens my door

My legs slide around
My feet find the pavement

He should be angry about how jealous I've become
But Asia is right
Cody's eyes are confused

Which makes me feel even worse
About how I've been
Acting

SOMEHOW

It doesn't seem
      right
          to let my hand
      slide
   across the
Space
I've created
   When I know he wants to pull me close

I wish I knew how many words it will take
To wipe away the hurt
My paranoia created

All this silence makes it hard to breathe
So I throw words
Into the still
I'm sorry I got so jealous.

Cody's face relaxes
He unfreezes his eyes from the straight-ahead place he's been
   staring
So I keep going
   I know you'd never—
   "Then why—"
   I don't know. I'm sorry though. Really sorry.
We keep walking
Balancing along the edges of the hole I created

"I don't know what your problem is lately," Cody says.
His voice sounds distant
Which is where I'll be if I can't make this right
    I don't know either, I say.
    "You've gotten so—" Cody stops walking and stares at
      the sky.
    Crazy, I finish.

Because maybe this is what crazy feels like
Having another version of yourself living under your skin
Another person who pops out at all the wrong times
Says all the wrong things

    "Crazy?" Cody's mouth starts to smile at the joke I didn't
      know I made
    Maybe.
    "Yeah, you're crazy all right. Crazy wonderful."

Cody reaches out and pulls my hand out of my pocket
We stop walking and face each other
"Just trust me, okay?"

And I do
Trust him
As much as I trust anyone

DISLOCATED

It isn't until we walk into the building
That I see Micah
Specifically
His arm
Cradled
In a sling

He and Asia
Are sorting through textbooks
Stacked tall in her locker
Her words rising over
The cacophony of the pre-A-block rush

"I can't believe you didn't call me!" Asia is saying.
"It happened pretty late," Micah replies.
Sheepish
As he hands her a physics text

"Or because he didn't want to tell her what really happened,"
    Cody laughs
        as we stop at his locker
        half a wall down from Asia's
What did?
        Cody spins the combination
        pops the door open with his elbow
        grabs a binder from the top shelf
"Kyler wrestled him out of her tree house," he says
        punctuates the statement with the slam of his locker door

"Missed the rope ladder and landed on his shoulder when he hit
    the ground."

It's not funny
When someone gets hurt
So I try not to smile
Mission impossible
Picturing Micah's little sister
Forever in John Deere boots and pigtails
Standing, arms crossed at the entrance to her tree house
The fortress Micah couldn't break

"Yep. That little girl kicked your ass, didn't she?"
Cody makes like he's going to pop Micah on the shoulder
As we catch up to him and Asia
Still sorting through books
"At least it's not broken," Micah says.
Cheeks pink
Now that I know how he got hurt
"Like dislocated is any better," Asia says.
"It is. I'll be able to rope again by the end of the month."

Really?
Because that seems so quick
Looking at his arm
Bound tight
To his side
"Technically, my doctor said anywhere from four to six weeks,
    depending on how fast I heal, so I'm giving myself three."
"If you start too early you're going to mess up your shoulder
    permanently!" Asia protests.

Cody and I hang back
Letting the two of them walk ahead of us
Asia telling Micah exactly what he should
And shouldn't
Do
About the shoulder
She can't believe
He wrecked

So what are you going to do?
Keeping my voice lower
Than I need to
Feeling like a jerk
For asking Cody about this
When Micah's the one who's hurt

"You mean for roping?"
Yeah. It sounds like he'll at least miss the first rodeo. Maybe the
second and third too.
"Doubt it. You know how Micah is. He's as good at being laid
up as nothing. I'm guessing he'll only miss the first one."
Are you going to sit that one out then?
"No. I—"
The warning bell cuts off the end of Cody's sentence.

Take two
"It turns out Kierra ropes. Heels mostly, which is fine because
that's what Micah did."
His words are running into each other now
Coming out one on top of the other as he tries to get them out
So she's your new roping partner?

"No. It's not like that. I'd never replace Micah. It'll just be for
one rodeo. Maybe two."

How very valiant
Drive by
Swerve to the side
Miss the point entirely
Which is this

Before I knew
Before even Asia knew
Kierra was clued in
Contingency plan set
Her skills called into play

Had Cody called her
After Micah called him
Completely bypassing Asia
And me?

We start walking again
This new information irons my voice flat
What am I supposed to say
As Cody kisses me on the cheek
Breaks away
Disappears into his class?

I stand
In a swirl of energy
People shoving books into bags
Dashing toward classrooms

As the secondhand ticks
'Round the clock

Thinking only this
    Leaner
        Lighter
            Faster
        Minus five
I can't let anything else
Matter

DOES IT MATTER?

Asia is done with this conversation
Before it even begins
She wants to ride
Barrel racers only tonight
Which means we have the arena until dark

Most of us
Including me
Are mounted
Warmed up
Ready to go

But she's running late
After having to scavenge through the tack room
In the horse trailer to find new reins
To replace the ones Scuba snapped when they slid off the saddle
    horn
Where they had been looped
As Asia was walking him toward the arena
The first time

"Seriously, Rae. I'm so done with the whole Kierra thing.
    Especially with the fund-raiser coming up."
Asia doesn't even look at me as she talks
Just pulls the latigo on Scuba's saddle tight
Runs her fingers along the inside of the cinch
Giving him a tickle and a pinch
Knowing how he bloats

Blows up his belly like a balloon
With the air he sucks in
Before catching her left stirrup with her foot
And swinging into the saddle

He exhales as soon as she settles in the seat
But she lifts the reins
Pushes him into a walk
Then a trot
    roll back
        side pass
    dismount
Before tightening the latigo
Again

Horses are funny, aren't they?
This is what I do
Topic switch
Swing the conversation around
When things get
Tense

"What?"

Asia stops now
Looks at me
With eyes that are less
Than amused
How they make themselves larger when they're getting cinched
    up. It's exactly the opposite of what people do, pulling in their
    stomachs as they tighten their belts.

"I seriously have no idea what you're even talking about
     lately."
Asia swings back into her saddle
Pushes Scuba into a trot
Toward the arena
I don't need to nudge her
Fancy just follows
Falls into stride alongside Scuba

"I meant what I said though, Rae. I'm seriously done with this
     whole Kierra thing," Asia says.
Not wanting to drop the topic
Until she has made
Her point
*I was just saying, it's odd how Cody had her all lined up to rope
     with him before either of us even knew Micah was hurt.*
"See, now I feel like you're trying to start something between
     me and Micah. I'm sorry you and Cody aren't doing well—I
     really am—but don't pull me into this."

Asia throws this last part over her shoulder
As she and Scuba cut in front of Fancy and me
Joining the throng of horses and riders
Loping around the arena
Along the rail

Fancy's ready to go
Champing her bit
Worrying it with her tongue
Eager to join the horses and riders
Pounding by

But I hold her up
Let Asia and Scuba get a bit of a lead

Making like the arena dust
Is the reason I'm rubbing my eyes
Burning
Red
With tears

ASPHALT GOSSIP

Everyone is always in such a hurry
Measuring the minutes
Dripping off the end of the second hand
At the end of the day

Only to come out to the parking lot
To sit on tailgates and
Lean against the doors
Of hand-me-down
Cars
To trade rumors

"You have to say something," Micah says.
"I've tried," Asia says.
I stop
Turn Sneaky Pete
As I wait on the far side of the truck
Out of their sight line
Because they sound like they're on the verge of a fight

    "I don't know what she thinks he's doing," Micah says.
    Asia's voice is a knife
    "Yes you do. Is he cheating on her?"
    "No, I'm just saying—"
    "Well, maybe you shouldn't."
    "Whatever. It's not my thing anyway."

It's my thing
With Cody
They're talking about

Cody and Kierra are?
Aren't?
Asia wouldn't be asking if she didn't have
Suspicions

The strap of my bag is cutting into my shoulder
I shift to adjust it
    tracing the edge of my clavicle
    noting how sharp it has grown
Forgetting the Diet Coke
In the pocket on the side of my bag
That falls out
Hits the pavement
Rolls under the truck
Hits the heel
Of Micah's boot

He leans down to pick it up
As I walk around the truck
"Diet! You can keep this one," Micah says as he scoops it up
   and hands it to me.
Thanks.
"I'm off," he says.
Leaning into Asia for a kiss
That she ducks

"What are you doing tonight?" she asks.
"Why?"

"I have to track down barbecues."
Micah looks at her blankly
"For our fund-raiser?"
"I can't. I have to—"
"Whatever. Get out of here," Asia says mock mad.
"I'll call Kierra. We'll get it done."

Or me
I think
You could call
Me

MY SHARE

Some people
Rev their engines
Fly out of the school parking lot
Not Asia though
She takes it slow
Coasting through the maze of people and cars
As I cue up the music
For our drive home

Thinking that I should thank her
For standing up for me
Because that's what it was
Wasn't it?
Her
Standing up
For me?
But not knowing how

It hate that it's like this
I should be able to ask her
Talk to her
About anything
But now…

I wait
Until we're on the road
To say
I can help you if you want. With the barbecues.
Realizing I've done absolutely nothing

To help with the fund-raiser
So far
Realizing that I haven't
Been asked to
Either

Asia slows
As she turns off Main Street
Onto the county road
We'll follow
Until the pavement
Turns to dirt

"Sure. That would be great. I probably shouldn't throw
    anything else at Kierra. It's not like she doesn't have enough
    to worry about."

Why? I mean, what's she worrying about?
Asia looks at me funny
Like I should know

"She's running for queen too. There's a ton you have to do
    to get ready. The speech. The test. We have to know
    every single NHSRA rule there is. Then there's the whole
    interview. I don't even want to think about that part yet."

I didn't know you were doing that.
"What do you mean? We talked about it."
Did we?
I'm not trying to be smart
Because I really can't remember
"Yes! And I tried to talk you into doing it, but you said no."

I remember that conversation
A bit
But didn't think she'd committed to running
Yet

Not that it took Asia long to fill the space
I left
With Kierra
Asia's new lunchtime buddy

Which means that maybe
Asia hadn't been sticking up for me
At all
Maybe it was Kierra
She was defending
Kierra who wouldn't
Even if Cody
Wanted

Asia rolls down her window
Holds her arm out
Parting the sunlight streaming past
With her fingers

I follow suit
Rolling down my window
Staring at the fields rushing by
Shamrock green
Thanks to the sprinklers
Chinking rainbows of water through the air

Not saying
    Anything
At all

PLEASURE READING

I read cookbooks now
Mostly at night
Standing at the kitchen counter
Next to the stove where a mason jar filled with bacon fat sits
   crusted to the range
Runoff from the morning strips Dad cooks cast-iron crisp
Bachelor's seasoning for any and every dish

Running my index finger along the columns of ingredients
Exact measurements
A quarter
Half
Whole
Cups of ingredients peeled-pared-ground-extracted-pureed
Into custards and tarts
    stir-fry and pastas
Grams of fat
    saturated and un
Proteins-carbohydrates-calories
Listed in user-friendly reference tables
Making it easy for me to prepare those Tuesday dinners for
   daughter-dad nights

They aren't as easy now
With our smiles stretched tight
Trying to bridge the space I left between our words
That seem to be falling away with the pounds
And I don't know what to do

To fill the holes
Because I don't know how they got there in the first place

Leaving me in the dark
At the counter
Hoping
Praying
The spaces don't get bigger

Wondering
How come
Asia never called me
Even after I offered
To help

SET-UP

I wish it were just this
The setting-up part
Without the event
If it were
I wouldn't have to change out of my jeans and
Into a dress
Tonight

Asia hands me a tower of tablecloths
Still wrapped tight in the plastic
Stamped with the dry cleaner's logo
"I'll follow you with centerpieces," she says
Before heading back through the clubhouse doors
To gather the mason jars
Turned flower holders
Made earlier today

Everyone else on the team is either done with their tasks
For now
Or running around
Doing errands
That keep cropping up

Leaving me
If just for a minute
On the patio
Already decorated by the lights
Cody and Micah picked up from the hardware store

Strung from the gazebo to the patio
Around and back again

I set the tablecloths
On a rough-hewn bench
Next to a planter
Shirking my duties
                    for a minute

Long enough to walk down to the creek
Dancing around the rocks
That shadow the pollywogs
Asia and I used to love
To catch

The loam of the bank
Turns my knees damp
As I kneel
To see
If they're still there
Nascent amphibians
Halfway to land
With their tails and legs

I think about the little girl
Who used to wave her hand over the water
The shadow of her palm
Scattering the pollywogs
She was always too nervous to catch
Worried she'd accidentally crush one
In her clumsy hand

Certain
Even then
She'd ruin
Everything beautiful
She touched

WARDROBE MALFUNCTION

I don't have that many dresses to choose from
Two to be exact
Only one of which will work
The red one with ribbon around the hem
That dips in the back
Comes out from the recesses of my closet
Onto my bed

Then the shoes
Heels or flats
A nonjudgmental
Forever supportive
Second opinion is what I need
Blue!

The sound of dog paws
Scritch-scratching against the wood floor
Followed by a groan
Blue's head pops out from under my bed
Where he has been gnawing the antler
He found behind the machine shop last week
Less chewing and more helping, please.

Blue smiles at me
Ducks back under
To grab the antler
Prongs worn down to nubs
Before he wiggle-worms the rest of the way out

Blue stands at attention
His tail twitching
    as I hold out the first pair
        then the second
Showing that he loves both shoes equally
Which isn't much help

    But then again
    I'm asking for advice
    From a canine
    With an antler
    In his mouth

My hoodie and jeans come off
The dress goes on
I look over my shoulder
Into the mirror on the bathroom door
And tug the zipper
Into place

The fabric that should hug my body
Drapes and gapes
In all the wrong places
Even with the zipper up
Revealing what my baggy clothes
Usually hide

Panic
Rises like helium
Makes my throat go tight
Because there's no way

I can wear this
Not tonight

But underneath
There is adoration
For the bones
I can see
The muscles
I can feel

Leaner
Lighter
Faster
Minus five

I'm closer
Than I knew

QUICK CHANGE

"Are you ready?" Dad calls up the stairs.
Almost. I just...
"What?"
I broke my zipper.
A spontaneous excuse
Knowing I can't wear this dress
Tonight

Dad's boots echo on the stairs
Because there isn't a zipper
The multiplier on his belt
Can't fix

I yank the dress over my head
Shove my legs into my jeans
Arms back into my hoodie
My hands do it
Before my mind thinks
Yank the zipper
Hard and fast
Leaving the fabric
Frayed where it used to run

A courtesy knock
And my bedroom door swings open
Dad steps in
Sees me standing
With Blue at my feet
My dress in my hands

"Let me see this thing," Dad says.
Exhaling a low whistle
As he runs his thumb along the zipper
I know he can't fix

"Do you have a plan B?"
No. This was the only dress I had that would have worked.
"Pants?"
Dad knows the answer
By the look on my face
"Pretend I didn't ask."

It's stupid
Because now I'm crying
Really crying
Over this dress I didn't even love
Leaving Dad to shift his weight
From one foot to the other
Hating problems like this
Ones he knows he can't fix

"Maybe your mom…" he begins
Pausing as he
Hears how present tense
These words sound
"In her closet. There might be something that would work."
Dad chews his bottom lip
Wondering if this was the right thing
To have said

I wonder if he knows
How I used to crawl into her closet

Closing the doors behind me
To sit on the floor
In the dark
With the smell of her

I'm not small like that
Not anymore
So I haven't looked lately
Which doesn't mean I don't remember
The color of every skirt
Every dress
Hanging there

My breath does a stutter stop in my throat
As I inhale and nod my head
Wondering if anything
That belongs (belonged)
To my mom
Will fit
Me

PERFECT

I chose
The dark blue one
Because it hangs a little longer
Looks a little funkier
Than something I'd normally
Wear

"You look beautiful," Dad says.
His voice catching
On the memory
Of Mom
In this dress

He opened the door for me
Helped me into the truck
Shooing Blue off when he tried to climb into the cab
Still letting him come
He just had to put his muddy paws
In the back
Where he prefers to ride
Anyway

Cody says it too
"Beautiful!"
Giving a low whistle
As he wraps his arm around my waist
Walks me to our table

Wearing this dress
That fits me
Just right

MOTHER-TO-BE

Calving makes the young ones nervous
Switching and straining
To catch a glimpse
Figure out
What
Who
Is making their bellies roll
    kicking back the light and the air with hooves spongy
      and soft
    from inside their aqueous utopia
    purgatory

But not Angel
Cut out and pulled into the sun after her mama sighed bubbles
    of blood
Crumpled dead outside the squeeze chute with her neck bent
    wrong
Leaving behind a bummer calf
Now come old enough to be a mama herself nine times over

"Gives us real nice calves," Dad says.
She's a sweet old thing, I add.
    When folks ask
      Eyebrows raised
    Why you hold on to that old cow anyway?

With them not having seen Angel
    A knock-kneed calf butting and begging for a bottle
    Growing strong

Even after coming out so still that the breath had to be
    blown into her lungs and the warmth rubbed into
    her limbs by the man who'd cried when he'd cut her
    out from the mama with her neck bent wrong lying
    in a heap of blood and mess
Standing proud and quiet
    Next to a seven-year-old in a ring lined with sawdust
    and the air smelling like livestock and heat and
    cinnamon crisp elephant ears—with a blue ribbon
    pinned to her leather halter
They don't know
So they ask

I've been there for every birth
Sometimes sitting on a fence
Others cross-legged in the grass
Or like tonight
Sitting in the truck
Watching
Waiting
For the calf to slide out into the world

Which is why tonight
I put my dress on a hanger
Shoved my legs into my jeans
As soon as we got home
From the tri-tip dinner
That earned our club
More than we ever thought
A single fund-raiser could make

And volunteered to sit
Beneath the stars
Listening to Salida Spring's only radio station
Past midnight
When the disc jockey goes home and the prerecorded playlist
     comes on
Always the same songs
Same order
Wildfire chasing down Miss American Pie

Blue doesn't mind
Neither do I
Sitting in the ranch truck with the heat rattling the chaff and
     dust in the vents
Watching Angel in the headlights
Standing calm
Waiting
Not missing the freezing cold that bit the calves' ears round last
     year
Teddy bear ears
Iced their bellies tight to the ground before they could stand

Not like this year
With the ground starting to spring green
Where Angel will lie down
Lick her calf dry
Nose it bleary-eyed and wobbly to its feet
Born natural and easy
Just as it should be

WRONG

That isn't how it goes
Angel groans
Strains
Her tail goes up
A hoof pokes out
There should be two
All I see is one

I set my mug on the dash
Grab the calving chain coiled on the floor
Please let it be two. Two hooves. Two, two, two.
Out of the truck
Over to the pen
Where I see that it's not

It's one hoof
Where two should be
My coat is off
On the ground
The sleeve of my flannel shirt rolled up so I can reach in to feel
What my hand shouldn't be tracing
The line of the calf's hips, not the head
It should be the head

*That number, minus five. Stay up, Angel. Keep standing. Minus
five.*
Catch the hooves
Legs in my hand

Loop the chain around
Minus five.

Angel's straining and bawling
I'm pulling
Pulling on the chain
Wrapped around the legs of that little baby calf
Coming out wrong side first

Minus five, minus five.
Pulling as hard as I can
But it isn't enough
My shoulder, bracing against Angel's hindquarters
She's going down
Lying down on the ground, groaning

That calf has to come out
For her, for it, this little life, these little lungs running out of
   oxygen
That calf has to come out
The chain thunks against the dirt
Sprint back to the truck where Blue's still waiting
Minus five, minus five.
The truck turns over once
Twice
It starts up
Pulls forward
Close enough that I can jump out
Loop the chain around the bumper

I've only done this once before
Dad was here then

Please Angel, don't die, don't you dare die, not even for your calf.
I sprint back to the truck
I'm next to Blue
He's sitting tall in the passenger seat
Watching Angel too
Watching me ease the truck back

So much metal
So much weight
Attached to a calf still learning how to breathe
Pulling back
Back until the calf slides out
Hooves, hips, shoulder, and then the head
The baby calf lying on the ground
*Minus five, minus five. How long is too long? The calf is lying so
     still, too still.*

Blue's right behind me this time
We're out of the truck, on the ground, next to the calf
Which turns out to be
A boy
Wet and tired from the work of being born

I slide the chain off his legs
Angel turns to meet him
She noses him
Welcomes him with her tongue, warm and wet
Cleans off his face, around his eyes, inside his nose and ears

This one wasn't easy
Not the way it should be
But she did it

We did it
Angel and I

I'm just glad
That number on the scale
Minus five
Helped keep me strong
As long as I was repeating it

MACARONI

Should not be the primary art medium for anyone
There isn't anything creative about nonperishable food items
That's what they're using every time I come in though
Macaroni

Tuesday
They pasted it to construction paper
Today
They're stringing it onto ribbon
Pasta jewelry
They'll wear home

Lacey only used four pieces of elbow macaroni
No paint
She pushes the macaroni pieces end to end
Slides them around and around her wrist

Which book should we read first? I ask.
Lacey shrugs
How about this one?
I pick up a book from the top of the stack between us
There's a picture of a cow on the front
Painted in honey and brown watercolors
Do you like cows?
Lacey lifts her eyes from her bracelet to meet mine. "Yes."
Her wax-paper whisper saying what it knows it should

The plastic cover crinkles and gaps at the spine as I open the
    book on my lap

I'm so tired
Everything is heavy
I want to curl up on one of the beanbags
And sleep
Lacey's eyes are back on her bracelet
I hate this cow already

BY ANY OTHER NAME

Page two
Sticks to page three
I don't even want to know why
More cardboard words I can't bring myself to read
We have this cow named Angel and she had a calf a couple of weeks
*   ago. It's a lot cuter than the cows in this book.*
The words just fall out of my mouth and I feel stupid
Like I just initiated show and tell

Lacey stops train-car pushing her macaroni bracelet around her
    wrist and looks at me
"What color is it?"

Her voice sounds strong
The honey and brown cow book slides off my lap as I sit
    forward
He's all black except for above his top lip. He's got a little bit of
*   white there, so he looks like he's got a milk mustache.*
"You could name him that."
What. Milk?
"Yes."
Lacey looks at me, waiting for an answer with those eyes
I want to memorize
Before they look down to her shoes again

I love it, that name I mean, Milk.
"Do you think he will?"
Who?
"The baby calf. Will he like the name Milk?"

Lacey climbs out of the beanbag chair that has nearly
    swallowed her up
Sits on her knees facing me
He'll love it.
I may be the owner of the only beef calf in the county
Maybe in the world
To be named after a dairy product

Lacey pulls one of her braids off her shoulder
Adjusting the ribbon at the end
I wonder where all this serious comes from as I watch her
Trying so hard to get the loops in the bow exactly equal
Lacey pulls
The ribbon comes undone

My hands reach through the space between us
Toward the ribbon I know I can tie just right
But she jumps back
Lacey gathers the books into a pile
Shoves them back onto the shelf

Lacey faces me
Looking at her shoes
Balls up the ribbon in her fist
Her knuckles go white
Holding it so tight

"Thanks for reading to me."
Her voice is flat again
Thanks for naming my calf.
Lacey nods
Bites her lip to keep away the smile that tries to grow again

Letting me know that at least that part was right
Telling her about Angel

Maybe I can get it right again
Next week

WILD TURKEY

Elbow to elbow with Asia
Inhaling air that tastes like spring
Legs dangling off the tailgate
Kicking shadows with our boots
Watching Cody and Micah
Arguing with the pipe coming out from the windmill

They yank their ball caps off
Kneading the sweat-stained bills back and forth
Staring into the rusted metal stock tank
Dry
As the ground trampled hard around it

Asia links her arm through mine and pulls me off the tailgate
"Thought we were going to shoot," she whines.
Bored by the chalkboard sky
Yawning
Above us
Guilty with the memory of Cow's nose
Pressed into little squares against the screen door
Scared to be within an acre and a half of a gun

Cody pulls his long barrel off the gun rack
A Remington
Same as the name of his horse
And I'm popping the truck box open
Tossing Cokes to Asia and Micah
Pulling out boxes of ammo
Stacking them on top of the hood like building blocks

Micah ducks inside the cab
Cursing the cold as he punches the glove box open
Pulling out a revolver
So chunky it may as well shoot caps as bullets
Antique handed down from his grandpa
    the kind that's meant to be used
    not just looked at

Since nobody wants to waste bullets chasing sagebrush
We stick
Plastic spoons
Handles first
Into the earth
Targets
And take turns
Laughing at the dust devils

Until a wild turkey steps out
With a stiff-legged strut
From behind a sagebrush
Let me show you how to do it right.
I taunt
Cajoling the gun out of Cody's hand
Knowing I could never hit it
Even if I tried

Movie star, gunslinging, gangster-style
I blow imaginary smoke off the end of the barrel
The last birthday candle
Extinguished
And wink at Cody
Staring up the length of my arm and over the gun

At that turkey strutting across the pasture
Running away from the shadow
Dragging long from his heels in the afternoon sun

Slowly
Gently
Pulling the trigger
Back
Relishing the tension
Of an Achilles tendon
Beneath my finger
The weight of the gun in my hand
Recoiling
Kicking
My arm up
Harder than I anticipated

My heart stops
My knees melt
Because I've shot cans and posts and sticks and spoons
But never the life out of something
Until now
When that strutting turkey is flat on his side
With blood
Running from where his head used to be
Turning the dirt black

Micah and Cody crow like they shot it dead themselves
Scooping it up
From the pile of feathers
That exploded around it
Because they can't hardly believe

That I blew its head clean off
Micah pulls his butterfly knife out of the pocket of his coveralls
Ready to gut it

Asia says we should have us a bonfire
Break out the Wild Turkey to go with the real one
Cody can call back to the house on his cell phone
Tell them we're not getting back till dark
But then he'd have to say the part about the windmill still not
    pumping
And the stock tank still being dry

So the turkey goes in the bed of the truck
And me and Asia onto the tailgate
Leaving Cody and Micah to argue with the windmill

Sitting there looking at the turkey
Lank in the bed of the truck
I think about that rattlesnake Dad killed
Back when I was little and he and I were out fixing fence
Cut its head off and buried it
Before he threw the body into the bed of the truck
For a snakeskin hatband

But that snake wouldn't die
Thrashing around
A writhing strand of Medusa's hair
Ramming its bloody stump
Against the tailgate

Angry

Fighting
To hold on
To the life
It wasn't ready
To leave

DRY

Cody stares at the windmill
A metal flower against the sky
The clouds exhale
Silver petals shiver
Cody keeps staring
"Come on," he says quietly.

Asia's off the tailgate
Feet on the ground
Next to me
She glances at her watch. "Are you getting hungry?"

What?
If she's joking she should be smiling, but she isn't
"It's almost dinner you know, that thing people eat around
    now..."
The water glunks out of the pipe in fat spurts
Splashing into the stock tank

"Yes!" Cody shouts. He sprints over and catches my elbow in a
    square-dance turn
Cody's feet stop dancing. "You coming over for dinner?"
Sorry, I can't.
I duck around Asia's "whatever" look
Because what does she know?

My Dad's making dinner tonight. I said I'd be home.
I can't remember if he said he was or not, but it doesn't matter
"Your loss. My mom's making shepherd's pie. I'm so glad we

got that windmill working." Cody says as he and Micah start
  throwing the tools in the bed of the truck
"We were so productive today, I can hardly handle it."

It was a productive day
A fine day
I walk around to the cab
Dad will be home for dinner, and it will be good
Perfect actually
I'll make sure it is

DINNER FOR TWO

Dad actually is home
Really is cooking dinner
Even picked up flowers at the store on his way home
Pink carnations wrapped up in baby's breath and tissue paper
Because it's his turn to treat me
After missing so many daughter-dad nights

He's had to work
Which has actually been fine
Because it's not like I'm a little kid anymore
I understand him
Being gone

Dad passes the food to me before he takes any himself
French-cut green beans
Salad to go with the steak
"So are you and Fancy ready for next week? First rodeo of the
    year."

I pass him the beans
Drop a few to Blue
Who snuck in from the porch to lie under the table
Blue alligator-snaps them up before they even hit the ground
My dog
The vegetarian

I think so.
I'm afraid I'll jinx myself if I tell him how ready Fancy and I are

How our runs have been setting the pace at practices and
    haven't been beaten
"Blue and I'll be there. We'll even get Uncle Tyler out of bed,
    won't we?"
Dad leans down
Ruffles Blue's ears.

Maybe it's the image of them sitting up in the stands next week
Dad's brother, Uncle Tyler, my aunt, and cousins
Waiting for me to ride
That gets me going
I talk about school and Cody and Asia
I even tell him about Lacey
Dad smiles around the vase of flowers in the middle of the table
    as he listens to it all

Blue stands up under the table
Walks over to the door
Asking to be let out into the evening that's fading into purple
That's how fast all this time with me and Dad has gone
Dad lets Blue out and steps
Into the kitchen for a cup of after-dinner coffee
I'd be having one too
If I were done
Eating
Which I'm not

TRULY

The knife is heavy in my hand
Pressing into my steak
Slicing off pieces I can't swallow
Could swallow
If I'd stop thinking
About the bone
That the muscle
That's now my steak
Once clung to

I just keep cutting
Cutting it into bites
Smaller
Smaller
Small enough to swallow

I was so busy with the weight of the knife that I didn't notice
How the space grew too large for Dad's words to fill
Leaving him to stare at his plate
At the clock
Anywhere but at me
Cutting
The pieces of my steak still smaller

Dad sets down his coffee cup
Moves it a few inches to the left and then back to the right
"It's okay. You don't have to eat every single bite."

He won't look at me
It makes me want to cry
So I smile
   Guess this means I'll have leftovers for lunch tomorrow.

Blue scratches and Dad pushes away from the table. He opens
   the door for Blue and begins to gather up the dishes. He's
   breaking the rules, because if he was the one who cooked, I'm
   supposed to be the one who cleans.

I stand
Pick up my plate and silverware
Follow Dad into the kitchen
The teeny sliced meat goes into a Ziploc bag
And Dad starts putting the leftover food into plastic-lid
   containers

"I'm sorry I haven't been around too much lately, Rae."
It's okay.
"No. It's not. I've missed you."
He folds me into a hug that makes it okay
Truly
Okay that he was gone
Now that he's here

PHOTOGRAPHIC MEMORY

Erase ya' Raesha
Or
Race ya' Raesha
He'd always say
That freckle-faced kid Danny
With his shirt that was never clean
Clutching that same brown lunch bag to his skinny chest
Never once switching out for a new bag
With clean creases and smooth sides
Just kept using that same brown paper bag
With its peanut butter stains on the bottom
And its sides worn fuzzy thin
He'd thunk me on the back with his same lunch sack every
    single day
As he walked past me and Asia to his table in the cafeteria
Which wasn't far enough away
After lunch—at recess, "I'll race ya' Raesha."
Get it
Race ya' Raesha

Or he'd sit on the other side of the classroom
Holding up his pencil
Pointing its eraser at me
Waggling it back and forth
"Too bad I gotta' erase ya' Raesha,"
He'd say

There he was
That freckle-faced kid Danny
Staring back at me from a second-grade class picture
I'd forgotten how he didn't have any front teeth that year
Nine gone at once
Right after the dad nobody in town even knew existed
Moved into his mom's house with the paint peeling away from
   the windows

Then they were gone
First his teeth
Then Danny
His mom too
All in the same week
Leaving his just-come-into-town-dad
Staring out the screen door
At the sky and dust
Which was all they left behind

But a picture of Danny
A kid from a memory half-forgotten
Wasn't what I was looking for
In the shoe box
With the photographs spilling out the top

What I wanted
Needed
Was a picture of my mom
One where I could see the color of her eyes
Because after hearing for forever that my eyes are the same
   color as hers

I woke up tonight on the couch
After my TV show had melted into snow
And the white noise filling the living room made it hard to
    breathe
I jerked awake
Scared
Angry
That the edges of my memories
Of my mom are withering gray
And maybe my eyes aren't hers at all

So now
With the glossy photos spread all around me on my quilt
Falling off my bed onto the floor
I've got to see-remember-know
For certain
But I can't find one
A picture of my mom and her eyes
And all the pictures of me and Dad
        Asia and my cousins
                my aunts and my uncles
Are making me cry harder
I don't even know when I started crying and my hands started
    shaking
But they are
The pictures and the tears sliding together

Until I find it
The one of me and my mom
Both in bare feet and shorts on her horse in front of the barn
Not caring that Rocky didn't have on a saddle

Or that our summer tan legs were sweating on his sides
Just sitting there smiling out at the camera
With our eyes
Just the same

ALARM CLOCK

"I tried to call to let you know, but you weren't home,"
Cody says as he walks around the horse trailer to meet me.
I was there
I was just taking a nap
Making up for the hours I missed last night
When I was busy sorting through pictures and dreams

For some reason, falling asleep is a lot easier
After the rest of the world has been jerked awake by their
    alarms
That's when I can sleep
Did sleep
In the middle of the afternoon while I was waiting
For Cody to pick up Fancy and me for rodeo practice

It doesn't matter if I was there or not though
Because I didn't know Kierra was riding with us
Until he pulled up to my house in his truck
With her in the front seat
Oh.
It's stupid, but that's all I say
Oh.

"She's getting a ride home with her cousins." Cody lays a
    whisper-kiss apology on my cheek that smells like cinnamon
    gum and swings the door to the horse trailer open.

I try to hold on to that cinnamon-gum kiss
Because even in the afternoon half light in the trailer

I can see how thick the yellow-gold chest is
How well muscled the hindquarters are
On this horse that's anything but young
Anything but green
In a leather halter heavy with silver
Standing sideways and unfamiliar

Fancy steps in
Nosing and blowing at the soft-eyed buckskin
Standing where she normally does
Alongside Cody's bay gelding

I loop Fancy's cotton lead through the metal slat horse window
Step out of the trailer
Fancy looks so small
Breyer horse tiny
In her purple rope halter next to the buckskin

"You're okay with this? Giving Kierra a ride? I mean, she has
    to get to practice. Otherwise how are we going to get some
    timed runs in, right?"
A gust of wind catches the trailer door as I go to close it
Turning it into a metal sail that knocks me back a step
Cody moves to help
But I lean into the throb
That will grow into a purple-black bruise on my shoulder
And shove the door closed

"That had to hurt."
Cody pulls me into him
And we walk to the driver's side of the truck
He opens the door

Swoops his red ball cap off his head
Bows low
Pseudodebonair
As I step past
To climb in

MORE THAN A CHANCE OF RAIN

Staring out the windshield
I have the sensation that the truck is standing still
    that it's the fields-road-barns
               sweeping past
If it weren't for Cody's hand on my knee
I might fly through the window
Disappear into the clouds
Pressed flat on the edge of the afternoon storm
That we may or may not see

Kierra's gaze flits from me
To Cody
Out the passenger window
"Do you think it's going to rain?"
"It doesn't matter. We'll practice in the indoor arena if it does,"
   Cody answers.

And he's off
Talking about the precipitation that didn't come last year
Or even the year before
Cody loves weather
He always has
He built a rain gauge out of a glass soda bottle and a cork
It makes me feel better
Remembering how Cody let me try out his rain gauge
When we were in the third grade
Before the rest of our class saw it
The rain gauge
Kierra doesn't even know existed

"Technically, this area has been in drought conditions for the
   last three years," Cody's explaining.
Usually I'd be interested
Or at least pretend to be
But today I don't care
I just stare at Cody's work gloves
Grease-stained
Muddied stiff
Lying on the dash

My body drifts
I lean against Cody
If she weren't here I'd relax into the postnap lethargy
That I can't seem to shake
And lay my head in the triangle dip beneath his collarbone
Where his chest slides into his shoulder

It would be easier to count the miles
Between the stick-figure minutes
On the dash
If I could just rest my head

LINES SHALL BE DRAWN

Cody looks down at his watch
He hates to be late
Not that we are
We just arrived with everyone
Instead of before

"Thank you for the ride, Cody."
Kierra talks right through me
Cody tosses a response over my head. "No problem."
"I'll have my trailer by next week," she says.
"Any time. Really it makes more sense for you to trailer in
    with us anyway since we're roping together. We should keep
    doing this."
Leaving me to wonder when Cody's apology to me
Turned into this
Any time offer
To her

That's what I'm thinking about
While they get out to unload the horses
Leaving me in the middle of the bench seat
Wondering how thick the line
Between
Any and every is
How I can make it wider

The driver side door swings open and Cody pokes his head in.
"Coming?"
He dives across the seat

Grabs my legs
Spins me toward him
His fingers dance up my calves
Tickle my knees

Quit!
I'm laughing so hard that's all I can get out
My legs jerk
My boots leave dusty sole prints on his white T-shirt
As I try to wiggle
Away

Cody's fingers keep tickling
As he pulls me out the door
My back arches around the edge of the seat
Welcoming the feel of his
Body
Hips
Melting
Into mine

My feet find the ground and we stand
Pressed together
My hands slide around his waist
To find the small of his back
Coming to rest
Thumbs hooked
On his belt loops

I relax into his hands
Moving up and down my back
His hands running up

Sliding down
Slipping underneath my shirt
His fingers trace my spine
Stop
At my ribs

"Whoa, Raesha—"
He steps back
Pulls his hands away
Please say something
Don't say anything
Ripping through my mind
Because I know what he felt
Why his hands stopped at the base of the bones
That he never used to be able to feel
At least not through my back

The xylophone rib cage that I love
That I hate
Right now
Because his hands are in his pockets

WELCOME INTERRUPTION

That's when I see her
Running down the stairs bisecting the bleachers
On the far side of the arena
It takes me a minute to recognize her
Outside of the hallways smelling like peanut butter and paste
It's Lacey
Running across the parking lot in a bright green sweatshirt

"Raesha!" she calls.
"Who's that?" Cody asks.
The little girl I read to.
Only she isn't
Lacey's a different kid
Away from the carpet squares and beanbag chairs
She's smiling

The gravel presses into my knees as I bend down to meet her
     with a hug
How are you?
"Good! My cousins brought me so I can see my sister practice.
     She didn't know I was coming so I'm a surprise!"

Kierra comes around from the other side of the trailer where
     she was tacking up her horse
"Hey, you."
"Hey you too! Are you surprised?" Lacey asks.
"Very. Come here."
Lacey runs over
Kierra hugs her hello before helping her onto her horse

I guess part of me knew
But didn't want to think
About this
Connection
Another link
Between her life and
Mine

Lacey grins down at me
Happy at being so tall
Wraps her hands around the saddle horn
Kierra weaves her reins over and under
Through her fingers
Stares at her cousins sitting up in bleachers
They're talking and laughing with their backs to Kierra
Now that they know Lacey found her

Asia and Micah come from behind the truck with their horses
Lacey's eyes fall to her shoes
"She is so cute!" Asia says, talking around Lacey to me
I wish she wouldn't
Lacey should be involved in a conversation if it includes her
*This is Asia. Her sister, Alexi, goes to the same school as you, only
    she's in first grade.*
"Maybe you could come over and meet her," Asia volunteers.
I love that idea
I wish I'd have thought of it myself
Do you want to, Lacey?
Lacey bites her lip and nods
If all these brand-new-to-her people weren't standing around
    she'd be smiling

She looks to Kierra for permission
"Tomorrow?" Lacey asks.
"Maybe." Kierra looks back to where her cousins are still
    talking in the bleachers
"Kierra, you should come too," Asia says.
Little sisters
Big sisters
Only child
Out

"I would, but—"
Kierra looks down at Lacey
Whose little girl eyes
Are anticipating
A no
"We'll talk to Grandma when we get home."
"Promise?" Lacey says.

Kierra and Asia trade smiles
Both knowing how little sisters are
"Promise. On or off?" Kierra asks Lacey.
"On."
Lacey pushes off the saddle horn and
Slides over the back of the saddle
Sits perched on the blanket
Kierra swings into her saddle
Lacey wraps her arms around her big sister's waist

It's funny
Because I still remember how it felt to sit like that
Exciting and safe all at the same time
With the horse moving under you

An adult anchoring you
Only with me it wasn't a sister
It was my mom

Cody doesn't look at me
So I don't look at him
Because we're busy
I'm busy
He's rushing
To get his horse tacked up
I've got to get Fancy ready too
Micah's talking
Asia's laughing
But we're hurrying
Cody is
I am
And it's fine
We're fine—he's fine—I'm fine

At least
That's what I tell myself

DANCING ON DIRT

She didn't know I was coming over
Judging from the way her arm went across her chest
Hand resting beneath the opposite shoulder
Rolling the spaghetti strap of her rose-colored tank top
Back and forth
Beneath her index finger
Stepping aside to invite me in
Clearing the way for Lacey
My teddy bear buddy
To run past and into my arms

Their grandma
Sitting at the kitchen table shuffling through the newspaper
Looking more like a ma than a grand
Wearing a green-striped shirt
And a smile
So wide it pushed dimples into her sun-pink cheeks
Blew a kiss to her grandbaby
So happy her girls had a friend like me
Having heard about all the fun we'd been having
Kierra and I
At rodeo practice
Lacey and I
With the books

Telling me to come by again
Only next time to stay
For dinner

Put some meat on those bones
Of mine

Promising her special casserole
The one with noodles baked soupy
Under a layer of crumbled-up potato chips
Smelling of onions and herbs
That graces the table of each and every church potluck
Warming the bellies
Souls
Of the sick
And the sad

Talking to their grandma
With Lacey pressed against my leg
I almost forgot
About Kierra
Melting into the door
Splintered around the bottom
So pale without her makeup
Standing there looking so young
And thin
A washed-out version
Of the girl
I see
At school

Staring past me
Out the door at the chickens
Bobbing and clucking
Strutting across the hard-baked soil
Spreading away from the front porch

So proud of their feathers
Red streaked with gold
They don't mind it
The dancing
On dirt

"Kiss," Kierra said.
Noticing that we were about to go
Bending down to meet Lacey's lips with her cheek
Reminding her to be good
Watching Lacey
Skipping through the chickens out to my truck
Swinging her ponytail
Tied high on her head
Back and forth
Loving the feel of it on her neck

I wave at Kierra
Who melted back into the door before we even pulled out
Knowing that she would wave back
Not at me
But at Lacey
Sitting proud in the passenger's seat
Legs stuck straight in front of her
Clicking the sides of her sandals against each other

She did
Wave
And I was glad
It was odd
This hating

Someone you knew nothing
And everything about

PLASTIC-CUP TEA PARTY

We used to play house when we were little
Asia and I
Dressing up
Asia's white patched cat
With the extra toes
Who drooled when she slept
Even when she was a kitten
Stumbling across the lawn
A tangle of baby doll dress and legs
Caught up in a knot she couldn't untie
Even with her extra toes

Asia and I tipping our plastic tea cups to our lips
One pink
One orange
Sipping invisible tea
Sweet as cloverleaf honey
Smiling purse-lipped
After our four-legged wayward child
Somersaulting through the grass

The same grass we're sitting on now
Drinking real tea
Watching real children
Lacey and Alexi
Popsicles dripping down their hands
Standing in front of the rabbit hutch
Looking at them
One for every day of the week

Alexi's pointing to Wednesday
Who Lacey thinks should be named Oreo
What with his white belly
Sandwiched between the black
That's his tail end and his front

But Alexi's patient
Understanding that Lacey's a child
A little kid
Needing some instruction
On rabbits
Holding them
Feeding them
Doing it all just right

Asia's rolling her eyes
Both of us smiling
Purse-lipped
At her little sister
Gesturing with her Popsicle
Patiently lecturing her student

Lacey looks through her bangs
At the rabbits
At Alexi
And back again
The seriousness of it all
Showing through
As she looks only at the rabbits
Never once at her shoes

For once it's not off-center
Asia's two
To my one
That comes with being an only child
The envy of siblings
Hating the squished-together bathroom mornings
The already worn clothes
Never understanding the weight of it all
The responsibility that comes
With being
Just
One

Watching Lacey
Cradle the back end and the front
Of the rabbit called Wednesday
Sliding her feet across the grass
Slowly
So slowly
With Alexi
Hovering alongside
Stroking Wednesday's ears smooth against his head
Talking her through each step
Slowly
So slowly
Until they reach us
Asia and I
Stretched out side by side
On the nubby green blanket
Slightly greener than the grass
Rolling onto our sides
Corralling Wednesday with our arms

Our legs
Smelling like coconut
Shining with lotion
Backrests for the girls

Maybe next year she can do it, Lacey tells me
4-H, just like Alexi
Get some rabbits for her own
Name them after the months
Because Alexi has all the days
And I could come watch
Her at the fair
Showing off her rabbits grown and strong

I love it
Her leaning against me
The weight of being just one
Gone

LUNCH LINE NEWS FLASH

"I guess I'm excited and nervous," Kierra says
As I stand between Asia and Kierra
In the cafeteria lunch line

It's hard for me to focus
On being annoyed
By the fact that Asia didn't bother to tell me
On the way home yesterday
This morning in the truck
That they had a phone call
An interview?
I don't even know
Something for the queen candidates

The smell of the meat
Hamburgers frying in puddles of grease
On the grill
Makes it difficult
To concentrate

"I just wish you wouldn't have backed out, Raesha," Asia says
Pulling coins and rumpled dollar bills
From her pocket
"You could have worked Fancy through it."
 referring to the way my horse jumps out from under me
 when the flags snap
 as the girls ride by
 horses stretched out
 into a full gallop

around the arena
as a part of the opening ceremonies
members of the court are required to ride
I could have. But not in time for tryouts.
"I don't know," Kierra volunteers. "My horse was bad with
flags too, but he's fine now."

Of course he is
I think
Wondering where she went
My best friend
Who would have rolled her eyes
At someone
As perfect
As this
Not so long
Ago

Asia's eyes
Are pushing me through the line
Because I forgot my lunch
That's what I'd said
"It's on me," was her reply.
Not knowing
Probably guessing
That I can't
      can't
   won't
Let that grease
Touch my lips

"You'll be there though, right?" Asia says
As she throws her arm
Around my shoulder
"Emotional support?"

    We're closer to the front
    Of this line
    That I can't be in

Of course. It's just—
    I look up at the clock
    On the wall
*I have to let my dad know that I'll be staying late. I better do that
now.*
    Backpedal
    Sidestep
    My way out of line
*He's working at the stockyard today. If I don't catch him now, I'll
miss him.*
    Which is a little bit
    True

Asia's eyes are tight
As she watches me go
Knowing that I'm not coming back
For the lunch
We both know

I'm not
Going to
Eat

UNEXPECTED OUT

I want her to say
Something
Don't want her
To say
Anything

About the fact
I didn't
Come back
After the call
I didn't
Make

But what she says
Is this
"Take notes for me, Rae."
As she flashes the pink slip of paper
In my direction
Before she sets it on Mr. Fisher's desk
Permission granted to do the interview
Fifth block
Rather than after school

Kierra is hovering in the hallway
Ready to sit
Side by side
Leaning in toward the phone
With Asia
For the conference call

That doesn't
Include me
Not that it did before

"Wish me luck," Asia says.
Luck.
I want to run over
Give her a hug
But I grab my book
Out of my bag
Instead
Because she's already
Gone

I hate myself for this
Two-year-old
Jealousy
Mine, mine, mine
As I watch my best friend
Walk out
The door

CAUGHT

I see them
Before I reach them
Asia and Kierra
Sitting on the tailgate
Of Asia's truck

Kierra is smiling
Asia is talking
Her hands dancing
Drawing pictures in the air
To go with the story
She's telling

I'm guessing they got done early
Opting to come out here
To sit in the parking lot sun
Rather than returning to the classes
They'd already been authorized
To miss

So how was it?
I ask
Trying to look like I have any idea
What the call was even about
Ignoring the way their conversation
Aborted
As soon as I approached

"It would have been awful if Asia hadn't been there," Kierra
says.
"Yeah, right!" Asia rolls her eyes
tempers it with a smile
"No, really. I totally froze up," Kierra says.
"At the beginning, but then you were fine."
"Because you helped me through it."

Kierra pushes off the tailgate with the palms of her hands
Tosses her bag over her shoulder
As her feet hit the ground
"I should get going, but thanks again, Asia."

"You're welcome. But seriously, stop thanking me."
"Fine. See you, Rae," she calls over her shoulder
As she darts away
Leaving me wondering
When she and I
Became nickname
Friendly

"So it looks like you made that call for nothing," Asia says.
What call?
"Exactly."
Asia slides off the tailgate
Walks around me
To the driver's side door
Jingling her keys in her hand
"Let's go."

My left hand
Slides around

To my back
Fingers counting
Vertebrae
Ignoring the way
The earth slips
Beneath my feet
As another hole
Opens

Between me
And
My best
Friend

FIRST ONE OF THE YEAR

"There's my girl."
I don't have to be close enough to hear Dad
To know that's what he's saying
Forgetting that cowboys tip their hats
Instead of waving
Like he does now
Standing beside my uncle at the concession stand
With Blue tail-wag dancing around his legs

I toss Fancy's saddle onto her back
Run the latigo through
Pull it snug
Wave back from the far side of the arena

My eyes swim
Seeing how proud Dad is
Knowing he'll be here for it all
In the stands
With Alexi crawling all over him
My little cousins too
Running up and down the bleachers
Full of sugar and sun
Waiting through the bulls and the steers
To see me run
Because he'd never miss this
First rodeo of the year

I cup my hands to Fancy's nostrils
She blows them warm

Limbers my fingers enough to untie her cotton lead from the
    trailer
Slide the bit in
Grab the saddle horn
Pull myself up and over
Into the saddle
This day
This life that maybe I don't mind being born into

WAITING GAME

Excitement starts to uncurl in my chest
Pushes my mouth into a smile
Runs through my legs
Happy energy that sends Fancy dancing around the trucks and
    trailers
Parked kitty-corner, crisscross, first-to-come, last-to-leave
Toward the arena where Cody, Asia, and Micah are waiting

Cody mounted up
Asia on the ground
Holding Scuba's reins
As Micah pins Asia's number to her back
Horses and the riders gathered at the gate
Where the talk starts to fly

This is what you do while you wait
Act like you don't care
Aren't looking
Sizing up the horses
Their riders
Pretend to stare at the tractor
That fills our noses with diesel
Raking and pulling the earth raw
Waiting
For the tractor to drag the arena smooth

Cody catches my elbow as I ride up
Pulls me over into a kiss
His red ball cap

Too lucky to take off
Switch out for a straw cowboy hat
Until just before his go

I lean back
Sit tight in my saddle
As he slides his hand down my arm
Over my elbow
Catches my hand
My eyes with that smile
That lets me know this game's coming
Forever funny
A tender exchange turned tug-of-war
Our elbows lock
And we throw our weight into opposite stirrups
Arms stretched tight

Usually I can hold my own
But I whiplash toward Cody
Almost come off

He drops his hand
I laugh
He doesn't
I should have stuck on
Been able to pull back
I know it
He felt it

FLINCH

I wasn't even thinking about the bruise
Didn't even notice I had one
Until this morning
It was a shadow then
Darker now
Almost black
This bruise
The one Cody's staring at
Asia's seeing
Micah's ignoring

"What did you do?" Cody asks.
I don't know. I guess I banged my arm on something.
It sounds so stupid, but it's true
I banged my wrist against the pantry door when I was going to
    feed Blue
But I didn't hit it hard enough to get a bruise like this
I didn't think I had
I get bruises a lot lately
Without even knowing
How

"Where are you going?" Cody calls after me as Fancy
    trots away.
I'll be back.

My eyes fall to my right hand
Palm down on the saddle horn
To stare at the part I hope Cody didn't see

The knuckle swollen and red
The half-moon bruise that shadows the back of my hand
The cuff of my coat slides down
It's gone
Invisible
Quick quick quick

What I need is another sweatshirt
The one I forget to get after I see them
In the back of the brand-new Ford
All teal and chrome
Sitting side by side on the black plastic truck box
Sides warped wavy by heat and use
Just sitting
Staring out at the sky

Until Lacey sees me
Jumps over the side of the bed
Skip runs over
Full of giggles and smiles
Cowgirled up in her boots and vest
I lean off the saddle
Grab her hand in mine and pull her up—around—behind me
"My sister brought me. Just me and her," Lacey says.
Tells me it's all right if she goes
With me

We turn to leave
But I look
Wonder why Kierra isn't cold
Sitting there without a coat
Proud girl gone

In the air that's still sharp
Elbows on her knees
Forehead pressed into her hands
Eyes closed against the something
The everything
That isn't there

PORTEND

The thing is
I need to get Fancy warmed up
Truly
I do
Because barrel racing
Comes right after
Team roping

So that's what I'm doing
Long trotting her
Around the field
That stretches behind the pond
In back of the grandstand

Feeling the adrenaline
Pour through my veins
That always comes
Just before a run

Fancy is champing at the bit
Foam dripping from her lips
As we chase the shadow of a hawk
Across the grass
Laid flat
For haying

Perfect cover for the mouse
That somehow
The hawk can see

Dropping from the sky
Talons turned daggers
Skewering its midday meal
Without ever touching down

It feels like an omen
This bird
Diving toward the earth
But a portent of what?
That part
I don't know

Fancy wants to move out
Transition from a trot
Into a lope
But I sit deep
Slow her to a walk

Still moving in the wrong direction
Away from the arena
Even though I can hear
Teams
Being called

First up
On deck
Ready to go
Static blurs the edges
Of the names as they funnel through the speakers
But I know Cody's draw is toward the end

Giving him
Giving me
Plenty of time
To get in one more lap

AN ACCIDENT

I'm trying to time it
So I don't have to see

    Cody and Kierra
    Their horses loping around the arena
    Shoulder to shoulder
    Shimmying their ropes
    In cotton-gloved hands
    As they warm up
    Rating the steers
    Hoping they get one that moves out
    But not too fast

But knowing I can't miss
Cody's first timed roping
Of the season

For some reason
It feels as if
I've been out here
Too long
Chasing shadows

Left leg against Fancy's flank
Pushing her hindquarters around
We finish a figure-eight drill
Moving into a straight line
Back to the arena

Applause
Metal clanging
Horses in the box
Steers in the chute
"Next up—"
I can hear the speaker clearly now
"From Salida Springs—"

A kick and a kiss
Push Fancy into a lope
Slowing down as we hit the edge of the parking lot
Where the trucks and trailers are parked

Just in time to see
Justin and Ty ride
Not a bad run
Aside from the broken barrier

Their five-second penalty
Nothing as bad as mine
Because Cody and Kierra rode
Before them
Cooling down now
On the far side of the arena

Where Asia and Micah
Were waiting
Congratulating them
On the run
I didn't see

TRANSPARENT

It is such a stupid thing to do
So transparent
But I don't care

Fancy and I trot over to the truck
Where a cooler sits
In the bed
Filled with snacks
To grab a Coke

Before trotting over to the far side of the arena
Where Micah is standing
The other three mounted
Cody and Kierra sitting
Feet out of their stirrups
Reins looped around their horns
Relaxed

Unlike Asia
Fidgeting in the seat of her saddle
Adjusting
Readjusting her straw cowboy hat
Shading her eyes as she looks in the direction of the arena
Where the truck
With the trailer
Carrying the barrels
Is pulling in through the gate

I'm too close to them
To turn back
Before I realize my mistake
I should have brought three Cokes
        because Asia won't drink one
        not before she rides
Instead of one
But what can I do
Now

"What'd you think of that head catch?" Cody asks
As I ride up and
Slide the Coke
Into his hand
"He turned that steer perfect, didn't he?" Kierra grins
Saving me
Without even knowing it

"Where were you, anyway?" Cody asks.
It makes me feel good
To know he looked for me
But guilty
Because I wasn't there
Back by the trailers.

Asia turns
Her attention pulled from the arena
By my words
Her expression is flat
And I know
She knows
I wasn't there

"It was a hell of a run," she says
Cutting me in half
With her eyes
I kick my foot out of my stirrup
Unbuckling the leather strap on my spur
Tightening it up a hole
Because it's easier to look at the metal rowels
With prongs sharper than my conscience
Than at her

Cody pops his Coke open
Takes a sip
Before handing it to Kierra
Who smiles
Head no longer in her hands
Like it had been
This morning

It's not like I'd take a drink
Since it isn't diet
But still
The fact he didn't offer
Makes me mad

"Definitely the best time I've had in a while," Kierra says.
   "Thanks to you."
Taking a drink
Without even looking
At the calorie count
On the side
Of the can

"Give yourself credit," Cody replies. "That was a nice heel."
Kierra shrugs
Actually blushing

> This whole love fest
> Makes me
> Sick

Asia picks up her reins
Turns Scuba on his hind
"Let's do this," she says
My cue to follow
Leaving Kierra and Cody
To share a Coke
Now that it's my turn
To ride

I glance over my shoulder
As Fancy and I trot after Scuba and Asia
Realizing
As I look at them
Kierra and Cody
Sitting so easy
Side by side
That it's hard to remember
Who I'm mad at

Is it her
Or is it
Me?

FEELING DAD'S ARMS

Around my shoulders
Hearing his voice so proud
Makes me wish I could draw this victory out
Forever

Dad holds the buckle to the sky
The curlicue engraving catches the light
A picture of a girl on her horse
Hair flying as they turn a barrel
Just like Fancy and I did

We rode through the slack
Made the cut
Taking the final run faster than I thought we had
Until the announcer called out our time
An arena record

Leaner
Lighter
Faster
Mission accomplished

Cody and Dad are on either side of me
Talking over the top of my head to each other
Breaking the day into eight-second pieces
Laughing about the bad
Reliving the good
As we make our way around the arena
Trucks and trailers pull past

First to come
Last to leave

I don't wave at anyone as they drive by
Can't take my eyes off the belt buckle in my hands as we walk
If I stare at it
Hard enough
I can forget what it feels like to sit
With your forehead pressed into your hands
Eyes closed
Against the sadness
You don't want to
Can't talk
About

MONDAY MORNING

I'd padded downstairs this morning
To find the coffee
Poured into the white plastic pitcher
Stained brown around the spout
A plate of eggs shrouded with a napkin on the table
Love you, Rae
He'd written it on the napkin in ballpoint pen
First blue
Then black
Because the ink must have run dry
That's why he always carries two
Sometimes three
In the breast pocket of his snap-button shirt

I bypassed the eggs
Yolks melted into the napkin
Oiling the paper clear
Reaching
Into the wooden carousel rack beside the toaster
Packed with spices and extracts
For the blue packets tucked behind the vanilla
Pouring the contents
Twice as sweet as sugar
Into the coffee

Blue's at my feet
The plate of eggs goes on the floor for him
He looks at me
At the plate

At me
Wondering
If this delicious doggie dream is for real

Go ahead.
My dog
The fool-proof vault
Pushes the plate with his nose across the linoleum
Vulches the breakfast that scares me
It doesn't scare me
Recheck mental thesaurus
Delete "scare"
Insert "interest"

I've been so good since Saturday
The belt buckle might be
Must be some sort of talisman
Because I'm on my longest stretch ever
Food-free
X hours
And counting

I SHOULD

Get ready
Go to school
But the thing is
Asia's truck
Won't start
She called
Let me know

I go for the coffee
A second cup
Straight up
Black
And onto the couch
Extract
The remote
From between the cushions
Flipping through the television channels
Balancing the coffee cup on my knees
Watching
Two boys rolling plastic tanks and trucks
Through a miniature army base
Lakes—sand traps—camouflage tents
Never mentioning how different the game looks
Played on the dirt floor of a barn

A trio of girls posing maternal
Cuddling dolls
Never mentioning how easy it is to lose
The miniature shoes-clothes-jewelry

Or how odd the dolls look
When they're half-naked
Falling forward onto their large chests
Unable to relax their heels against the ground

Coming to rest on the neighbor I wish I had
Curling up at the end of the couch as he slips into a cardigan
Ties his denim shoes
Welcoming me into his home with his nursery-rhyme voice
Showing me
His neighbor
A film flickering in a picture-frame screen
About how pretzels are made

I notice for the first time that the clock
Inhabited by the tiger wearing a watch
Has no hands
Freeing the trolley to come and go as it pleases
Never late
I wonder how attached Dad is to the gold arms
Circling the face of the clock above the stove
With pictures of cowboy hats for numbers

Somehow that neighbor
The one I wish I had
Gets me to thinking about Lacey
My teddy bear buddy
The thought of her sitting stiff and straight on a carpet square
Staring at her shoes
Pulls me off the couch

Sends me upstairs to get dressed
Not really caring what I put on
Even though my legs look bigger
Fatter
Are they?
I could
Should
Weigh myself
But the coffee in my stomach
Will register
As pounds

A sweatshirt over my head
Shoes on my feet
I won't weigh myself, because if I've gained
I'll be in a bad mood
I can't, won't, will
I am quick, quick, super quick
Into my bathroom
Onto the scale
And I'm down

Two pounds
Down
It feels so good
I'm so good
Flying down the stairs
Out the door
Into the ranch truck
With primer-gray doors and the vinyl-backed calendar stuck to
    the dash
A complimentary gift to Dad and me

Cattle sellers
Valued customers
Awarded a year in miniature

Looking into the rearview mirror I realize I forgot
To conceal
The circles beneath my eyes
To thicken-lengthen-strengthen
My lashes black
To smooth my hair
Rumpled by my pillows on the couch
Nothing a ball cap wouldn't cover
That a kindergartener would notice

Halfway down the road
With the dust and gravel blowing from under the tires
Shooting behind the tailgate in a plume of dirt and granite
Blue's head pops up
From the truck bed
Where he's been hiding
Laid flat in the middle of the soda cans and rope
Baling twine and tools

Teased to his feet
By the rumbling and the moving
Tasting the air flying by with his tongue
Lolling out the side of his mouth
Stump of a tail wiggling back and forth
Standing tall on the wheel well
Destination unknown

SAFETY FIRST

According to the numbers
On the clock
On the dash
I have a few minutes
To spare

My head
Started to hurt
On the drive in
So I duck
Into the drugstore

Walk down aisles lined with toothpaste and feminine hygiene
    items
Around the carousel displaying postcards
With scenic images of Salida Springs
        Or someplace that looks a lot like here anyway
        Kept in stock in case a tourist ever came through
        Not that they'd be entirely welcome if they did
And find the shelves
At the end of the aisle with
Plastic toy soldiers
Squirt guns
And yo-yos
That holds what I am looking for

Ibuprofen
Extra strength
    Because a minimalist
    I'm not
My hand grabs a bottle
But my eyes linger
On the first aid supplies
That fill the shelf
Below
Snag on the row of tiny brown bottles
Between the bandages and the gauze

"For emergency use"
The label reads
"To cause vomiting in case of poison"

I grab one
Plus a box of Band-Aids
Just to make it look
Right
This purchase
That now includes
A bottle
Of ipecac syrup

Not that I'll take it
I'll keep it on hand
Just
In
Case

The box of Band-Aids falls from my hand
Clatters to the floor
Perfect opportunity
To bend down
    look behind
Over my shoulder
To make sure no one sees
As I slip
This little brown bottle
Into the pocket of my Carhartts

The Band-Aids go back on the shelf
And I head toward the front counter
Hand in my pocket
Fingers wrapped around
This thing
I can't be seen
Buying

"Playing hooky today?"
Harley grins from beneath his ball cap
As he takes the cash from my hand
No. Just a late start. Truck broke down.
"That's no good," he says as he throws in a candy bar
                        for good measure.

"Something to sweeten your day," he says, chuckling at his
   own joke.
Twin
His black lab
Born the only dog in the litter
Comes around from behind the counter

Wiggles his stump of a tail
The rest of it left behind in a barbwire fence when he was a pup
I scratch his ears
Grab my bag

Walk out of the store
Secret
In hand

I BETTER

Lacey sits forward on the carpet in the reading corner
Wants a better look
At my belt buckle
I've pulled the bottom edge of my sweatshirt up
But she actually wants to hold it
I unbuckle my belt
Slide it through the loops of my jeans

Lacey lays the belt out full-length on the carpet between us
It looks so long that way
There are three notches
Worn wider
Darker than the rest
Small
    Medium
        Large

Extra small
Just
One
More
Notch

My jeans are slip-sliding down my waist
I roll the top down
Lacey notices and laughs
"Your pants are too big. You need to go shopping for some
    right size ones."

I guess. Maybe I should put my belt back on.
"Yeah, you better."

I better
Stay focused on
This goal
That's obviously
Paying off

SO BRAVE

Blood turns black
When it's dead
That's how Lacey describes it
Gently pulling the Band-Aid back
Careful to leave half stuck to her skin
Partially covering the scab
Where the gravel tore into her elbow
When the wheels of her bike went sideways
Throwing her against the road

That's what her scab is
Blood turned black
Hidden beneath an antiseptic strip of plastic
Decorated with black-and-white spotted dogs
Smooth as the beanbags crunching beneath our weight

Lacey smooths the Band-Aid back into place
Pressing it firm
Pointing out how her fingernails
Painted glittery and pink
Match the puppy's tongues
"It didn't hurt. Very much."
You're so brave, I say.

Did you do any art this morning? I ask.
Because I never ask what I'm actually wondering
If I did, I'd ask Lacey how it is
With Kierra
If she's the kind of big sister who hugs Lacey when she falls

Or the kind who finger-pokes words that make Lacey feel small
For not having been more careful

"Yes." She walks over to the table covered with papers lined up
    edge to edge
Four down, six across
I don't know why I remember that
But I do
The dimensions of a classroom table measured in construction
    paper rectangles

Lacey shoves her hands into the back pockets of her jeans
Looks for her square of paper
It's on the edge
The last one on the bottom row
She touches the paint with the tip of her pointer finger
It must come away clean
Because she picks up her picture
Carries it over

There is a black crayon line
Bisecting the paper
"Do you like ballerinas?" she asks.
I nod
Wondering why she's pointing
At the crayon image with her index finger
Pressing the tip into the chest of the caricature's triangle body
Suddenly caring more about this ballerina
With a featureless face and matchstick legs
Than her shoes

"Because if you don't like ballerinas, you can look at the
    rainbow."
She lifts her finger
But not her eyes
Pointing to the other half of the page
At the rainbow
Black and gray
Layered one on top of the other
I lay my hand on the page next to Lacey's
Covering up the rainbow with my palm
I love them. Both.

"Do you know what?" she whispers.
What? I'm whispering too
Lacey's hand finds my knee
Balls up a fold of my jeans in her fist
"I already knew about blood.
How it turns black when it's dead.
I saw it before.
On the rug.
Under her head.
My mom's."
Your mom—
    "She's gone."

Looking at her looking at me
With eyes that won't ever forget
All I can see is her scream
Hanging in the air
Falling
Because her mother isn't there to catch it

HOOKY

I watched my feet walk down the hall
Out of the conversation I broke in half
Without even meaning to
I just couldn't listen
Couldn't focus
On what Asia was saying

I thought I could
I intended to
Meet Asia at the door of the classroom
Fifth period
Where Kierra sits across the aisle from me
Blood turns black
Blood turns black
Blood turns black
Stop thinking

Instead I walked
Minus five
Across the asphalt
Minus five
Felt the sun on my neck
Minus five
My shoulders
Minus five
The small of my back
Minus

Rinsing away the smell of peanut butter and
disinfectant

Five

I rolled down the window in the truck
As I pulled out of the parking lot
Felt the wind
Sharp with dust

There were my feet
Stepping out of the truck
Out of my sandals
Across the gravel driveway and onto the grass
The wet cold of Blue's nose nuzzling my hand
Twisting and wiggling around my legs

When my hands find Fancy's neck
Rubbing her around the ears
The fingers threaded through her mane almost look
Feel
Like my own
Connected to the body
Straddling her back
Inhaling the grass and the sky
Moving toward the lake that's more like a pond
Edged with sand and silt

Feel the water climb up my calves
As we splash away from the shore
Step until the sand and silt fall away
Leave her hooves to churn the water and the emptiness beneath

Swimming
The water lifts my body off her back
To float

Here in the now
That is my arms
Moving through her mane
Swirling on top of the water
I can almost
Believe
This body
Is my own

HINDSIGHT IS BETTER

It's a flat-footed statement
An accusation
"You're okay," Asia says.

I'm okay.
Glad we're on the phone
Because I'm cleaning, cleaning, cleaning
Organizing my closet

"You walking out of school today is okay?"
 I'm sorry, I know I should have—
"People worry, you know, when you disappear. I mean, you've
 been so—"
 What?

My fingers find my collarbone
 minus five
Because I've been so
 minus five
Frustrated
That my closet
Is
So
Full

"Different lately. You just take off, in the middle of school, the
 middle of lunch. You never eat anymore. You act like no one
 notices, but—"

My hands move fast
Pull sweatshirts out of my closet
Send them flying
Across my room
Onto my bed
I'm not doing this.

"Of course you're not, because you're fine, right? Perfectly
    fine. And as long as you're okay, the rest of the world, which
    now includes me, can go to hell. Oh, except for Lacey,
    because she won't tell your secret, right? Little kids are pretty
    handy that way."

I look at the sweatshirts
Stare at the wall
At the ceiling
Because really
What does Lacey have to do with anything?

"I don't know what to tell you, Raesha,
but this is fucked
completely fucked
and I
don't
know
what
to
do."

INSOMNIA

It works best when I begin with my toes
Or it used to anyway
Imagining them relaxed
Pinky toe first
Pulling a blanket of sleep
Up and over my foot
Ankle
Calf

Eased into the rest that's abandoned me tonight
Sitting at the end of the couch
Knees pulled to my chest
Staring into the television
Ignoring the weight of the phone in my hand
Wondering (knowing) what Asia would say
If I called
Said I was sorry
Again
Knowing I could sleep
If I called
        Unless...

A HUNDRED REASONS

I would probably call
If I wasn't so interested in the television
Completely absorbed in the show chronicling a woman's travels
Through England-Iceland-China-wherever it was she was
I was suddenly on my feet
Nudging Blue with my toes
Not waiting for him to stretch himself awake
And follow me upstairs
To organize
Something
Anything

Last night it was cleaning the kitchen
The counters
The floors
Tonight my closet
Now the guest room
Not that a guest has ever stayed in it
There's really no need
What with the spare room downstairs
Much more comfortable than the guest room upstairs
Where no one has slept
Since Dad moved his clothes into the room down from mine
Because after she was gone it became too hard
To sleep there
Alone

This is my favorite place to clean
After the arms of the clock have swung into the single digits
When Dad is away
Working

Leaving me
To organize
This space
To sort
My thoughts

EVERYTHING IN ITS PLACE

Blue walks through the door
His nails clicking against the wood floors
The crankiness that festered all day
Like the cactus spines in the pads of his paw
I had to pull out this afternoon
Leaving him limping and sore
Fills up his chest
Escaping as a groan as he flops onto the floor at my feet
I kneel and kiss him on the muzzle
Smoothing his triangle ears against his head
Pausing to untangle a cocklebur from beneath his collar

The cleaning always goes the same
Beginning with the kerosene lamps
Lined up along the top of the dresser
One in each window
Lifting the glass off each
Rubbing it clear with one of Dad's old shirts
White cotton worn through
Fibers broken by the work
Of the hauling and feeding and moving that never ends

Next to the bed
Smoothing the sheets
I never asked where the quilt went
The one with the doves and leaves she was given
She lay beneath
For naps
That became longer and longer

I wish I had
Asked

Next to the floor
Running the dust mop around Blue
Beneath the bed
Where the handle
Catches the edge of a box
The size of a deck of cards
Tucked into the frame
Now laying in the fluff of dust
Pushed and piled by the mop

Clove cigarettes
I remember her quitting
Or trying
Forsaking those moments she spent with the stars on the porch
Beneath my window after I was in bed
Exhaling her way out of the day
Taking up walking instead
Around the pond
Through the pastures
Because she had a little girl who needed her healthy she'd said
Not knowing about the tumor in her breast
Already there
Growing
Slowly
Growing

That's where I go
To the porch and the stars
Blue sits on the steps beside me

Hindquarters perched one step higher than his paws
Nosing the box on my knees
Urging me to open it
And I do

I can see the box isn't new
A matchbook tucked into the plastic wrap
Top half-torn away
So I don't know why my hands start shaking
When I see they aren't all
There
Why the tears start
When I pull one out
Shorter than the rest
Gently snubbed

Blue backs away
Curling up on his saddle blanket
When I pull the flame through the tip with my breath
Feeling
Loving
The fire pouring down my throat
Running my tongue along my lips
Tasting the sweetness
I thought I knew

FALLING

He said my head bounced
Against the tile
When the floor pulled me down

We'd been hovering in the hallway
Just outside the classroom door
"Then how come you didn't drive together?" he'd asked.
We just didn't.
But he knew Asia and I were fighting
As soon as he saw her truck pull into the parking lot
Without me
Which made me mad
Because if he knew
Why was he asking?

I'd been standing
Back pressed
Flat
Holding up the wall
Holding up me
Talking to Cody
Absorbing the cool of the metal lockers

Had my knee not been locked
If I could have slept
Even with Blue tight against my side
Curled up underneath the blankets
His head smelling like pond water on the pillow next to me

I couldn't fall
Asleep

(I'd gotten the shakes
Bad
Last night
After)

It's a bad habit
Like biting my nails
Or moving my lips when I read
Only this one
This habit
Tinges the bristles of my toothbrush with blood
Filling my mouth with the taste of baking soda and iron

That's what I'd thought of
The pond
The way the water feels filling up my nose and ears
When I'd reached
For
Cody
There
Now

He wipes the blood
Trickling from my nostril
With his bandanna
Always tucked in his back pocket
Tender as a cow licking her calf clean

Me looking up
Surfacing
Through
All the voices

AFTERMATH

I sit
Stand
Am raised up by Cody
His arm
Around my waist
Holding me strong as I blink the walls slanting sideways right

I can't tell if it's the blood
Staining Cody's bandanna
The taste of baking soda and iron
On my tongue
Or the floor
Pitching and rolling
That makes my mouth fill with saliva
Nausea

Mr. Retsom steps out the door
Into the hall
Wondering at the commotion
That is now me
Leaning against Cody
Encircled by stares

Cody guides me through the audience
To the office
Where I lay
Inhaling the smell of coffee and ink
On the bed with the paper sheet and tablecloth-thin blanket
Listening to Miss Mary Lee typing at the computer

Monitor edged with photos of her children
School nurse
Secretary
My former babysitter
    back when I wore turtle-patched overalls
    not caring if my socks matched

Ice in the plastic bag
Pressed to my forehead
Melts
Finds a hole
Seeps
Through the washcloth over my eyes
Into my hair

I know I should go back to class
But the fear in Cody's eyes
Will have flowed through his lips
Into Asia's ears
Heart

I won't
Don't
Know what to do
About the trouble
I created
    again

EXIT STAGE LEFT

I'd stood at her desk
With the phone
In my hand
Stuck
Because
"Your dad's not home?"
Miss Mary Lee asked.

No
But he will be
Home
Soon
I said
Which wasn't much
Of a lie

"Well then. What should we do?" she'd asked.
Knowing I couldn't go back to class
Not with a headache like this
Knowing I definitely didn't want to wait
On the paper-sheet bed until my dad could come

Which is how I ended up here
Sitting in her car
The gas fume pop of the ignition
The crunch of tires on the gravel of the staff parking lot
Headed home

I wish I would have
Know I couldn't have
Talked to Cody
Found Asia to let her know
That I didn't
Wouldn't need
A ride home
Before I left

"Now, you'll be all right, won't you?" Miss Mary Lee asks,
As our driveway comes into sight
"Give me a call if you need anything."
I will. Thanks for the ride.

Blue comes tearing around from behind the house
In a plume of dust
He must have been dozing
For us to have gotten this close
Without him hearing

Miss Mary Lee reaches over and turns the music down
"I mean it. Any little thing comes up and you give me a call."
I will.
I repeat
But I won't
Feeling better
Now that I'm home

I swing the car door open
Careful not to look back
Into eyes that care

Too much
Thanks again.

I end up saying it more to Blue
Dancing around my legs
Happy to have me
Home

Miss Mary Lee leans toward the passenger side window
Still open
"Get some rest, sweetie," she calls.
As she backs out of our driveway
I pull out my best smile
Dust it off
Put it on
As I wave

Reminding myself
I am fine
I don't need
Anything
At all

STRIPPED BARE

Standing in front of the open refrigerator
Absorbing the cold with my body
I stare at the shelves
Lined with food
Dad restocked
Before he left last night

I haven't touched any of it
The food will all go bad
By the time Dad gets back
So what does it matter?

All of it
Goes
I'm not leaving
Anything
Juice
Cheese
Yogurt

The trash can is under the sink
I stack it full
Strip the shelves
Bare
Protecting myself
So I don't
Fuck up
Throw up

I've been good
My body feels clean

The trash can is heavy
I drag it out the back door
My arms are so tired that I can't lift it
Into our outside can
It doesn't matter
It's better this way
Throwing away one thing at a time

The bag is the last to go in
This is what control looks like
It feels good

ROLE PLAY

The trash can is easy to carry
Now that it's empty
Inside the phone rings

It's Dad
I knew it would be
School ended
Add drive time
Enter phone number
And here I am
He's on time
To the minute

Focus
How are you
  was school
Is Blue
And the cattle
How are they

Minus five
Focus
On filling my voice
With the energy I don't have
Because it's fine
It is
So that's what I say

His radio plays in the background
I picture him in his truck
On the map in my head
A red dashed line starts
At the X that is our house and crawls across the state
Dad starts talking
About this stockyard
And a registered Black Angus sale

I walk upstairs to my room
Phone cupped to my ear
To the pile of clean laundry
I threw on my bed this morning
Without folding
I'll do it
In a minute
Just not now

The sun teases me over with a warm square of light
Through my bedroom window
I see a truck
Asia's truck
Driving away
With Blue chasing behind

Dad's story is winding down
I pick up
The tail end
I've got to go.
Drive safe.
I love you.
I say

Miss you
I think

I click off the phone
Look around the living room
For some sign that Asia was here
That she came in without knocking
Like she always does
But she didn't come in
Didn't wait
Not even for a minute

DELIVERY

My books are
Stacked on the porch
Homework
Asia brought me my homework

Blue's twisting and wagging around my legs
My hand finds his head
My mind wanders back
To the food in the garbage
It would hurt
Filling my stomach
It would hurt
Jamming my hand down my throat
It would be good
To hurt
Like that right now

The dust from her tires
Still hangs in the air
I pick up a book

The one on the top is the biggest
The heaviest
An anthology
I love the weight of it in my hands
On my knees
As I sit down on the top step
Blue sits next to me

My fingers walk down the spine of the book
Grasping it on either side
It's a broom
A fan
Sweeping back and forth in the air
Scraps of paper
My notes
Flutter free
Floating for a moment
Before they hit
The ground

UNEXPECTED GIFT

It wasn't what I had wanted
That bike
Slightly more than lightly used
Cracked leather seat veined dark with age
Wheel spokes skinnied away
By the rust that colored the frame
But it was great
That's what I'd said when Dad brought it home
So excited to fix it up with me
That summer after seventh grade

I'd had to work at it at first
Shoving the magazine picture out of my mind
The one I'd taped to the bottom of my sock drawer
I knew it was too much
What with the tractor
Needing to be replaced
Too expensive to ask for
A bike like that

It's still there
On the bottom of my sock drawer
The picture edged with yellowed tape
Of the Sapphire Princess
White tires with saber-toothed treads
To crunch through the gravel in the drive
Tropical sea blue frame
Silver streamers fountaining out of the handlebars
I knew just how they would sound

Those metallic streamers
Snapping in the wind I would make

The best part had been the seat
Cloud white
With a picture of a butterfly
Pulling a ribbon of rainbow across the sky

The more we had sanded
    oiled
        primed
That old bike
The easier it became to see my butterfly
That old bike
Rattle-canned new
Named Ollie

KINETIC

My legs need to move
I don't run
But a walk wouldn't be fast enough to keep up with my mind
That won't stop skipping

Back to the memory
Of Cody
Looking down at me
After my head
It bounced
That's what he said

Back to Asia's truck
Driving
Away
Which is where Ollie comes in

It's been a long time
Since Ollie came off the wall
A mass of thistle twisted through her spokes
Leave itchy nettle bites across my knuckles
Up my arms
As I pull her free

Tires need air
Seat has to be raised
But the paint
Goldenrod yellow according to the can
Sealed out the rust that comes after the rain

Twisting up the seat is harder than I thought
Pollen slurries with dust
Solders screws stiff
It's worth it though
This getting her out
Ready for a ride
Because if anyone would understand
How I feel
It would be Ollie

Ollie knows what it is
To lie dismembered on the porch
Evening after evening
Listening to the night bugs bounce off the porch light
Wondering if you'll be put back together
If all the pieces will still fit

All I want to do is ride
Somewhere
Fast enough
To leave the confusion
Behind

WAKE-UP CALL

I shouldn't have gone back in
To grab my water bottle
But I did
Now the phone is ringing
I do
Don't
Want to
Have to
Answer it
Because what if it's
Dad

Hello.
"Raesha?"
Mr. Bradford. How are you?
"Good. I was calling because I heard you—"
Right now I hate this teeny, tiny town
Where news can't be corralled
For even a second

Got sick. But it's no big deal. I'm fine now.
"Glad to hear it. I've got to have everyone healthy you know."
I can picture him
Playing with the brim of his ball cap
Wishing this call was over
Almost more than I do
Because cowboys like him
Don't have conversations
Like this

"You haven't looked well…"
I've been tired.
My feet pace
Across the linoleum and back
Not liking where this conversation
    "I'm going to need you to get a doctor's note before you
        ride again."
Just went

What?
"It's a liability thing. No big deal."
But I can still come to practice on Friday, right?
"Sure. Just bring me a note."
All right.

Knowing that won't
Happen
I'll forge one
Before I go to a doctor
Who will get it all wrong
I'm not sick
I'm ready to ride

"Take care, Rae."

Flat line
Dial tone
Conversation
Done

BLACKOUT

Leaner
    Lighter
Faster
Minus five

This game
Isn't
Over
Yet

This person I'm watching
From far away
Looks a lot
Like
Me

Pouring cereal
Whole grain O's
Into the bowl
With milk
Lots of
Milk

Bowl
After
Bowl

Because I deserve
To hurt

Like
This

POISON CONTROL

It has been in my top drawer
This tiny brown bottle
Tucked into a roll
Of green and white socks
With tiny kittens on the toes

Two tablespoons
Should do the
Trick
So I drink
Four

Plus two
Not expecting
The maple syrup
Sweet
Taste

That makes me gag
As I pour water
Glass
After
Glass
Of water
Down my throat

Hands shake
Falling leaves
Frost melts

Into beads
Of sweat

Turns my skin cold
As my knees
Find the floor

Retching
Only water
From a stomach
Twisted
Torn
To
Rags

Blood runs
Turns my knuckles red
It's still
Not
Enough

When will
It will
Never
Be
Enough

ROLLER COASTER ROAD

It's called Roller Coaster Road
Not by any sign or map
You know when you're on it though
Taking the back way to town

All of a sudden the road starts to buck
That pounded clay road
Rises out of the flat
Tosses you up
Slides you down
Over and over

That's where I go
To the hills
That rise and fall
To the hills
Guaranteed to make
My muscles burn
My heart slam
In my chest

Guaranteed to push
My body
To the edge

ALL FALL DOWN

I pedal
Hard
Gaining momentum
Down the first
Hill

Losing it on the way up
The next
Standing
Weight in my heels
As I push the pedals
Around

Heartbeat thunder
In my ears
Muscles scream
Stomach cramps
Fold me
Over

Tires slow
Ollie's front wheel
Right angles as she clatters
To the ground

I fall
Heaving
Eyes streaming
Bile

In my throat
Blood
On my lips

The sound
Of a diesel engine
Louder
Coming
Closer
Registers

Gravel cuts
My palms
I drag myself
Toward the edge
Of the road

Dry grass
Against my cheek

Everything
Goes
Dark

911

I gather them up
First my arms
Then my legs
Straighten them
Bend them into being
Remind myself that they're still attached
To this body that's mine

That's up
Running toward the truck tipped on its side
In the grass on the far side of the road
Wheels still spinning
All I hear is her name
Lacey, Lacey, Lacey
In a voice that's not my own

It's hers
Kierra
Calling to the sister who won't open her eyes
Kierra lifts Lacey
Passes her through the window of the door dented shut
Puts her in my arms

I'm scared
By the blood above her eyes that should be open
Careful of her arm
With too many bends
As I set her gently, so gently
On the ground

Kierra needs me
I reach through the window
Our fingers twine
I pull
She climbs though the window
Into the fuel-soaked air

We have to chain link
Arm through arm
Not sure who is supporting-dragging-pulling who
Onto the grass

Lacey, Lacey, Lacey

I can hear the sirens
See the rescue vehicles in the finally that feels like forever
The trucks
One of them white
Wailing red
Loud enough to wake her

Lacey, Lacey, Lacey

Eyes thrummed open by the pain
Out of the dark

I
    fall
       in

NEXT PLEASE

It's my own reflection
Staring back at me
From the plate glass wall
Separating the waiting room
From the gift shop full of flowers

I look away
From the image
Of the girl I hate
Watch people in wheelchairs and casts
Move through the doors to the parking lot

Open
    Close
Inhale
    Exhale

Wishing the door to the ER
At the end of the hall
Would do the same

Kierra got to go in
Being family and all
Wasn't made to sit on an orange plastic chair with faux wood
   arms
That match the counter
The nurse in teddy bear scrubs
Sits behind
Fingers moving across a keyboard

Eyes locked on her computer screen

I can't look at them
Those fuzzy brown bears tumbling across her shirt
So I go back to looking at the bloody-lipped, bruised, stiff girl
Who looks a lot
Like me

IF ONLY

It's my fault
I dug them
The holes that our words fell into
Dad's
      Mine
Excavated the dirt myself
That I packed into balls and flung
At Kierra

Who wouldn't have pulled off the road
So hard
Too fast
Wouldn't be behind the red-signed doors
With Lacey
    My-her-our Lacey
    Lacey with her arm bent so wrong
If I wouldn't have been there
Been able to pull Ollie into the grass
If I could handle looking at the world straight

But I couldn't
Had to slant it sideways
Had to be light
The kind that comes from doing without
When you're trying to turn yourself into a shadow

I just thought
Maybe
If I could whittle

Strip away the part of me that
        loves-hates-cries-worries-wonders-thinks
Too much
The me that was left
Wouldn't hurt anyone

Wouldn't leave them lying in a bed
Breathing butterfly breaths
Until they're sent home
When the doctors know
What they don't tell you
That the needles running in
Can't replace
All the life
Leaking out

These calm, peach-colored walls
With the pictures of
            flowers-fruit-trees
Life turned still
I can't sit here
All my pacing
Sets the nurse glaring
I can't calm down
Not when I'm thinking about Dad

They told him I was fine
But Dad doesn't know
Won't believe
Until he sees me
So he'll drive too fast

Will forget how the washboards pull your truck
To the side of the road

Then it will be
My fault
Again

SPARE CHANGE

The nurse raises her eyes from the computer screen
Distracted by my pacing
Hands me change
She pulled from a drawer
Beneath the counter
"Why don't you get yourself something to eat?" she suggests.
"The cafeteria is closed, but there are vending machines."

I know where they are
Machines backed against a wall
Plastic fronts glowing
In the room
The size of a closet
Next to the elevator

I remember this place
    "Get yourself a treat."
    That's what they'd said
    Aunts, uncles, neighbors
    Handed me quarters
    Clustered around Dad
    Fenced him off from the doctor coming down the hall
    In his paper pants
    Mask pushed down around his neck

I begin at the end farthest from the door
Cokes, ice cream, coffee
It doesn't matter
How much

What it is
One machine, then the next
Punching the coins into the slot

The best part is the sound of my palm
The sound of it slapped flat against the buttons
Smooth rectangles
Small round knobs
    pop open the skin, pulled white across your knuckles
        curled in a fist
    if you hit them
            just right
I pretend it's my fist knocking them out
The cans
    bars
    cups
Rattle-clunked down the belly of the machines into the trays

It doesn't take long to get a rhythm
Build up speed
    whack, rattle, clunk,
    whack, rattle, clunk, *fat*
    whack, rattle, clunk, *worthless*
    whack, rattle, clunk, *bitch*
    whack, rattle, clunk, *fat*
    whack, rattle, clunk, *worthless*
    whack, rattle, clunk, *bitch*
    whack, *fat* whack, *fat* whack, *fat* whack, *fat*
    whack

"Raesha—"
Daddy—

I stop
It all
Right then
Crying and crying until my chest is empty
With his arms wrapped around me
All the pieces
    I thought I'd lost
Come together

WAITING—STILL WAITING

I know it's still there
The scared
That filled her eyes
Spilled down her cheeks
Left riverbeds of red
When she'd heard
It was them

Pulled from the crumpled cab
Coughing bile and blood
Stretched out backboard-straight
With latex gloves

How will she do it?
Corral it
Inside her chest
Where a grandma's heart beats

It's what I worry about
Sitting curled into Dad
In this space
That tastes like bleach
Waiting
Worried
Waiting
Wondering

When her eyes will turn to slate
If they haven't already

Beneath the exam room lights
Where she holds one up
The other lying down
Two sisters
Her life

How will she
Could I
Forget
Forgive
The cause
This worthless waste
          of a girl

WHY CAN'T THEY SEE?

All that scared
Seeps through the cracks in my heart
Fractured
As her arm

Lacey
My Lacey
Their Lacey
Sterile gauze pale
Holding her arm
Set straight
Broken—so broken
Even Dad's arm wrapped around my shoulder can't hold me
Together

The jagged sobs send the pieces of me flying
That don't understand why they're not mad
Those three sets of eyes
One's arm wrapped up tight
The others by her side
Fortresses around the wheelchair
That wasn't meant to hold her
Not Lacey
      My Lacey
Their Lacey

"You saved us," Lacey says. "Got us out."

This is worse
Than the slate
Not this kindness—
It's not right
Their grandma's garden-stained hands hugging me limp
Kierra
Butterfly-bandaged cheek pressed against mine
Hugging me too

Why can't they
Don't they see?
It was me
All me
The why, that's the we, in the now, standing here

Can't they see her?
Broken—so broken
Here now
Like she was then
When we were the fortresses
Dad and I

Dad's arm reaches through the hole
Time left behind
To pull me close

And I know
Dad sees her too
Can hardly see past
The ghost
Who was our life

SINK OR SWIM

"It wasn't your fault—
You know that," Dad had said.

Those words were easier to swallow
Almost made it down to my heart
As I'd stared into the rearview mirror
Watching the hospital shrink
    small, small, small

Caught in the half-moon collarbone groove
Of my neck
Those words woke me up
Made it impossible to breathe

Drove me out to the porch to sit
Gathering stars
Around my shoulders
Tracing tiptoe solar systems on the stairs

Until I see it
Frame scratched
Otherwise intact
Against the side of the house
A Good Samaritan's deed
One better left undone

My shadow pulls me
Across the dry grass
To the truck for tools

Wrench, screwdriver, nails
Hammered one at a time into the tires
My bike
Coming undone

First one nut
     Then two
Wheels, handlebars, seat
From the frame
Rattle-canned new
Forever ago
Thrown into the bed of the truck
By hands slick with oil

The keys drop from the sun visor
Into my lap
As I slam the door against the night
Drive through grasshopper leg music
Out to the pond

Where I Frisbee-throw them in
Tires
Handlebars
Catching
Pieces of metal
Of me
Sinking into gone

NEWS OF THE DAY

Cody didn't even know
It had happened
Until he drove into the parking lot this morning
Where the words hit his windshield
"Heard your girlfriend almost died yesterday," they'd said
As they grabbed books and bags out of their rig
Parked alongside Cody's rusted-out, dented-in orange truck

Cody didn't stay to ask
Swung out of his truck
Walked into a run

Blasted into the cafeteria
Through the line of heavy-eyed students
Doing the breakfast shuffle
In one door, out the other
With waffle sticks

Scared me so bad
Asia too
The way his gaze was flying around the room
Until he found us
Saw me

He'd been out of town
Should have called
Didn't know
"What happened?"

So I tell him
Around the plastic stir stick in my mouth
Worried flat between my teeth
About the crumpled metal
Ice-cube words
Leave me cold
Even the warm coming off my coffee
Can't make it disappear
All that cold

That pulls my eyes into my coffee
So much easier
Than thinking about the part
    the ipecac and the purge
    the food I should never
    have eaten
The part I never told
Anyone
About

The guilt will wake me up
Tonight
    Tomorrow
And again
Until the forever I don't have to think about
If I let myself grow cold

But they won't let me
Not Cody
Tipping my chin toward the light
Or Asia
Hand on mine from across the table

Holding me down
Lifting me up
Willing me to blink
Back into my life

HALLWAY CONFESSIONAL

Dodging the shoe squeaking-jostling-growing, moving energy
That fills the eight-minute space
Between last class and next
Kierra walks down the hall
Comes right up to me and starts talking
All chitchat
Cast aside

"I thought you'd been hit. You were just lying there. Crumpled
    next to your bike," she says.

> The rest of the world falls away
> Leaves me standing
> Across from her
> On this island
> Of accountability

I fell. I guess I—
"I was driving too fast."

Kierra charges ahead
Shoving my excuses out of the way with her words
> "It makes Lacey laugh when I fly up and down those hills.
>   She's so tiny she bounces all over the place, even in a
>   seat belt. I know it's not an excuse, but that's why I was
>   driving like that. I just love hearing her laugh."
Kierra pauses
Clears her throat

"Before our mom killed herself, she used to do it all the
    time. Laugh. You know?"

And I do
Not exactly
Because no one's lives
Are exactly the same
But still
I think I know

"Anyway, she saw you. On the ground. I jerked the wheel,
    slammed the brakes. My front tire blew, and then we were
    rolling. She was crying. And I couldn't help her. Again. But
    you could. You did."

Kierra, I—

"I should be mad at you. At myself. I don't know. I don't even
    care. All I know is, if I were to lose Lacey, I might as well die
    myself."

We stand there
Looking at each other
Me and her
Because those last words
Came so fast
So hard
They knocked the breath
Out of me

"Sometimes I hate it here," Kierra says.

But she's not angry
Just sad

"I miss everything back home. My school. My friends." She
pauses. "My dad. I really miss my dad. But we can never go
back. It's just too…"

Her voice melts

Sad.
I finish for her
Without even thinking
Immediately wishing I could take
That word
Back

But she reaches out
Pulls it in
Exhales and nods

"It is. Don't tell anyone I said that last part, okay? About
hating it here? Everyone has been so nice to me. They
might feel bad if they knew, and they shouldn't. It's me.
Like I said. I miss my old life."

And everyone who was in it
I think

"Anyway, here."
Kierra digs in her bag
Pulls out a construction-paper star

With a crayon picture on the front
A girl and a dog
From Lacey to me

Tell her I said thank you, I say, taking it from her hands. *And I
    hope she gets better soon.*
"I will."

Kierra pauses
Turns to go
But stops
"I hope you do too."

I look down
At the star in my hands
As the bell rings
Wondering just how much
She
And everyone else
Knows

SPECIAL DAY

I don't know why
I didn't think this would be awkward
I just didn't expect them both to be here
Kierra and her grandma Jean
Standing alongside me at the edge of the carpet square
Beneath the dancing numbers and animal cracker alphabet

Behind the audience of seventeen kindergarteners
Eyes trained on the one standing beside Miss Dixon
Wearing a smile
Holding the Sharpie
That each of her classmates will use to initial the hot pink cast
Encasing her arm

Because that's what she has requested
On her Special Day
An uppercase, proper noun, double-decker date
Lacey's first day back
After three days out
And her birthday
Six years old today

I knew her birthday was this month
I'd just forgotten when
It makes me sick
To realize that I've been so
Self-absorbed

Lacey ran up to me when I walked in
"I missed you!" she'd cried.
Her voice so strong
Soaring above the shadow of the little girl
With sun-streaked braids
Who had been so interested in her shoes
Forever ago

It made it worse to know that Kierra and their grandma Jean
Had seen the package in my hand
And assumed that the horse-print wrapping paper
Curlicue ribbons
Meant
I remembered

Because it never crossed their minds
That it had been meant
As a get-well-please-forgive-me gift
Another day of just her and me
Sitting on the beanbag chairs the color of lima beans
Just me and her
Or so I'd thought

"Can you stay for my snack?" Lacey had asked
As I handed her the gift
That's what I'm thinking about now
    as the kids all stand
    ready to single file past Lacey
    so excited to sign her cast
That snack
Caramel Rice Krispies Treats
Individually wrapped

One for everyone
Including
Me

INSURMOUNTABLE

These are the things I can do:
    Ride a horse
    Rope a steer
    Drive a tractor
    Buck a bale
    Fix a fence

This is the thing I cannot do:
Eat
The
Rice Krispies Treat
In my hand

Knowing
I should
If I could
I would?

But my mind says
Not this
Not now
Not even for Lacey

Because
There is a wall of numbers
Stacked
On the side
Of the wrapper

That wall
It's too tall
Too thick

I can't make it
Around

SHOULD-WOULD-COULD

The next part should be easy
Here is how it should go

I would understand
Why
I should
Eat

I would see
How sick
I
Am

I would know
That this (eating)
Is the right thing
To
Do

If I admit that I can't
Couldn't
Do this
Not even for Lacey
I would have to admit

I am
    out
       of
           control

CHEESE SANDWICHES

He made them
Dad did
One for each of us
An after-school snack
On matching blue plates
Because he came home early today
To check in
To make sure
I'm doing
Okay

I thought I'd have
More time
Before this discussion
More time
To figure
Out
How to
What to
Say

But this sandwich
In front of me
Is making it difficult
Impossible
To speak

Dad sits
Sinks

Into his chair
Across from me
At the kitchen table
Hating myself
As another hole opens
Yawns and stretches wide
Between us

I wish I could tell him
Why
This began
How
It will end
But I can't
Because I don't
Know
So I stand
On the far side of the hole
Staring at my sandwich

"It's hard, isn't it?"
His words
Soft and slow
I nod
Because it is

He raises his sandwich
Takes a bite
Tips his head toward me
Glancing at my sandwich
As he chews
Slowly

Slowly
Just one bite
Then puts his sandwich down

This sandwich
It's only cheese
Two slices of bread
I can do this
One bite
I can
And I do

Chewing
Slowly
  Slowly
Just one bite
Then I put it down

This is how we go
Slowly
  Slowly
He and I
Ignoring the tears
On our cheeks
As we eat our sandwiches gone

FOLLOW-UP EXAM

We need to check in, Dad said
Make sure everything is okay
What with the accident and with you
Being so thin
Too tired
Just not able
To
Eat
Not like you used to

Even though
As I pointed out
I did
Eat
That sandwich
Yesterday
Which he knows
Because he saw

But still
This is fine
It makes sense
A trip to see
What is wrong
If anything is
Which I doubt
       pretend not to know
   it
      is

ON SECOND THOUGHT

Seeing this doctor
    the one who handed me red suckers after my booster shots
    pasted Bugs Bunny Band-Aids over my playground cuts
    who hugged me hard after Mom
    was gone
Hadn't seemed like a bad idea
At first

But now that I'm here
Sitting in the waiting room
Jiggling my knee
Staring at the *Highlights* magazine in my lap
It does
Feel
Bad

The door to the hallway that leads to the exam room opens
"Raesha, come on back," Kami, the nurse in Snoopy-print
   scrubs, calls.
I look at Dad
Wish we could call it off
But we're here
With my name
Hanging in the air
A smile on Kami's face
As she waits

Come with me
The words are in my head

But Dad reads them with his eyes
Reaches over and squeezes my hand
Knowing there are some things
Dads can't do
Exams rooms are one
Not for a daughter
Growing out of her teens
"I'll be right here," he says. "See you when you're done."

It makes me feel better
Hearing him say the words
Knowing
That he
Will
Be
Here

SLIGHT VARIATION

I got on the scale
Backward
Which was fine

Wore a blood pressure cuff
Made for a child
Which I loved

Was shown that my nail beds
Were slightly blue
Which I knew

Saw the mercury in the thermometer
Hover a few degrees too low
Which made sense

Since I'm cold
Sitting here now
In a paper gown
Watching Dr. Larsen write
In blue ballpoint ink
On a chart

She looks up at me
And sighs
Her mouth smiles but her eyes
Are sad
And I know
That she knows

My secret
Is
Out

DOCTOR'S ORDERS

It's Dad, Blue, and me
Three across
In the truck
Headed back home

There's an orange file folder in my lap
Full of pamphlets
With pictures of laughing kids
One a picture of a plate
Full of food
With the words—
    "Food is Medicine!"
Across the top
I hate that one
The most

Stapled to the inside of the folder
Is a business card
With a phone number
And an address nearly two hours away
A referral has been made
To this therapist

But
It's the loose-leaf pages
Behind the pamphlets
That make me nervous
Meal planning sheets
The exchange system

Dr. Larsen had explained
No calories
Foods lumped into groups
Grains, fruits, vegetables, milk, meat, and fats
Eaten at each meal
Fill in the blanks
On the sheets
Showing how many exchanges were consumed
Simple as that

Dr. Larsen made copies
Thirty
One per day of the month
Then what? I'd asked.
"Then we'll see," she'd said.

Which made me mad
Because we both know
What we'll see
If all these blanks are filled

Me
Fat

THE QUESTION

So can I ride? Mr. Bradford said I need a note.
I'd asked

"No. Not now anyway," Dr. Larsen had replied.

I'd known
By the look in her eyes
There was nothing
I could've done
To make her
Change
Her mind

"Ask me that question in a month," she'd said.

I asked
But the truth is
I shouldn't compete
Even if I can—
At least not this year

I have no right
To try to follow
In my mom's footsteps
Not after
What I've done

DAY ONE

Breakfast
Looks like a shake
Tastes like chalk
Viscous as paste
Clogs my throat
With this glut of calories
We call a
Supplement
That sits in my stomach
Heavy
Like
I
Am
Now

GONE

I've been thinking about it
All day
Using the downstairs bathroom instead of mine
Avoiding
The scale
Dr. Larsen banned
That Dad doesn't even know I have

But I'm thinking about it now
Hidden away in the cabinet beneath my bathroom sink
Because Dad is out at the barn
Leaving me
A choice

Which it really isn't

I go upstairs
To get a shirt
Possibly a book
It doesn't matter
I go
Upstairs

Blue pads behind me
One step, then two
Through my room
Into my bathroom
Because, really
It can't hurt

Seeing a number
On a scale
Just once
      Cross-my-heart-hope-to-die-promise-myself
Just once

Because as long as it didn't go up
Even if it didn't go down
I need to see
Have to know

Even with the memory of the fuel-soaked air
Sirens slicing the sky
And Lacey's arm
      Bent so wrong
I still want to
Need to
Know
Hating myself for being
So weak

My fingers flutter
Butterfly wings
On the edge of the cabinet door
I open it
Band-Aid rip—quick
To see

There's an empty square on the cabinet floor
Where my scale should be
Not that I need it
I remind myself

That scale
Because I don't
Not anymore

But the electrical storm in my chest
Explodes
Wires snap
Sparks fly
My elbow hits the wall
Plaster and bone
It hurts
I'm glad
I can cry
About this

I slide down the wall
Knees to my chest
Cradling my elbow
In the palm of my opposite hand

Blue slinks in
Settles down on the bath mat beside me
Leans in to catch a tear
As it slides down my cheek
With a swipe of his tongue

That's when I see it
A plain white note card
Cut into a teeny tiny square
With a pink felt-tip heart on the front
Scotch-taped to the inside of the cabinet door
Above where the scale

Should
Be

I grab it by the corner
Peel it off
On the back it reads
     It is time. Love you, Rae.
          —A—

She shouldn't
Love me
Asia
That is

I know
I don't

LEFT UNSAID

Asia called
To say hi
To talk about

    School
        So much homework, possibly a quiz. Then there's that
           lab, the one she didn't do
    Rodeo team
        We're traveling—next week—next month—we should
           probably check. Both of us ignoring the fact that I'm
           not allowed to ride yet.
    Alexi
        She makes her crazy. That goofy little kid.

My stomach
It hurts
But it's easier
Not to think
About
That
When I listen
To Asia talk

All the food
In my stomach
From lunch—dinner—snacks
All I do now is eat

Flopped on my bed
Staring at the ceiling
My thoughts wander between her words
I wonder how long it will take me
To fall asleep
Tonight

There's a dance
Asia's saying
Never mentioning the note
Or the space
Where my scale
Used to be

I hate (love) you
Why did you do this
To (for) me
My mind shouts
As I listen to her talk

"I've got to go," she says. "Talk to you tomorrow."
Sure.
But then I grab
The end of the call before it falls
Thanks.

The night sky opens up on the line between us
Quiet and dark
We sit there
For a moment
She and I

"Just don't—"

I know. I'm sorry. I won't.

"I've missed you."

Me too

I think

Me

Too

PRESENT TENSE

Dad isn't gone anymore
At least not at night
We play cribbage
He and I
After we make dinner, that is

I lay the plates down
He serves the food
Tonight it's stir-fry
Spicy beef and bamboo shoots

It would be hard
Without the cards
Even with Dad here
It would be hard
To follow through
With the meal

But the game makes it easier
Dad sticks the pegs into the board
I'm red
He's blue
Always the same
Which I like

Dad wiggles his eyebrows
"Ready to lose?" he asks.
A smile on his face
As he deals the cards

Hands of six
Discard two
Everybody needs to have a dream.
Because that's how we do it
Tossing down challenges
Alongside the cards

It's easier not to think about the food
On my fork
Crossing my lips
Touching my tongue
When I'm thinking about runs and straights

Fifteen-two
Fifteen-four
Some nights are easier
This isn't one
And a run for seven
It's the rice that's throwing me
Water helps
I lay my cards down
Take a sip

Dad's go
He's got the crib
That's what I think about
As I take a bite
How he just jumped ahead of me
By twelve

This might be a two-game meal
Make that three

Because his crib is good
Very good
He's going to bring it home
Fast

But it's fine
His winning
And we'll play again
Hand after hand
Until this meal
Is gone

EXIT STAGE LEFT

For some reason I didn't tell Cody
Where I'm going today
But Asia knows
It's embarrassing
But I couldn't keep it
From her
The fact that I have to see
A therapist today
Right now
To be exact

Ducking out at the end of second block
Leaving fifteen minutes early
So I can meet my dad
Parked out front
Next to the flagpole
Staring through the windshield
As he runs his fingers
Up and down Blue's back
While he waits
For me

Standing in front of my open locker
Staring at the collage of pictures
Papering the door
Asia and me
Cody and Micah
A picture of us
All four

Where did she go?
That girl in the middle
Who looks a lot like me
Or at least the me
I used to be

I shove some books into my bag
Not really caring which ones
Just knowing that
Homework
Is something I should do tonight

"Hey."
I jump
Turn around
Asia
Hall pass in hand
"Thought I'd come and wish you luck."

I want to cry
Smile instead
As I shrug my bag onto my shoulder
Thanks.
She twines her arm around mine

I bite
The inside of my cheek
Knowing that if the tears start to fall
I might drown

We don't really say anything
She and I

As we walk down the hall together
I'm so grateful
For her

Knowing that
Even when I try to
I'm not going through this
Alone

THE GREAT UNKNOWN

I'm going to hate her—
The therapist
I've been pulled out of school
To see

I'm not going to talk
I've got nothing to say
Except that I'm mad
About the food
I'm always eating
    about the fact that my stomach
    always hurts
        I'm mad at this body
        I can't
        control

"You ready?" Dad asks
As he pulls the truck into the parking lot
Of this brown building
That could be any building
    It's that nondescript
But it's not
We're two towns and a world
Away from home

Sure
I say
Easy as anything and swing out of the truck
But not before I'm certain my window is down

More than a crack
For Blue
Who I wish I didn't have to leave behind
Because this would be so much easier
If he could come
Too

I shut the door
Gently
Letting my fingers sneak back through the window
To scratch him around the ears
And it's this
The way the he cocks his head
Looks right at me with those eyes
One blue
The other brown
That breaks
All this ice
Inside
Me

I can't
Don't want to
Do this
Any of this
Anymore

All the talking-thinking-feeling-hurting
That has become my life
I shouldn't think
Would never say this out loud
But it was easier

Then
When all I had to think about was
That number
Minus five

Dad's hands are heavy
Warm on my shoulders
As he turns me
And we walk
He and I
Into this

Another moment
I know
Nothing
About

CEMENT WORDS

I'd like to start out by telling her
That people like me
Don't do
This

Therapy is for girls
Who like to talk
About themselves
Who wear heels
Not boots
Who drive a car
Never a truck
Who couldn't tell a heifer
From a bull

There's a clipboard in my lap
A pen in my hand
Boxes on a sheet to check
Answers to questions
Do I feel sad…
    Happy…
        Disempowered when…

It's easier to look at the questionnaire
Than at this woman
Sitting in a chair
Across from me
"Call me Taryn," she says.

Taryn sitting
In this space that looks more like a living room
Than an office
With its caramel-brown couches
End tables and lamps

Taryn is thin
Not the kind I am
Younger than I thought
She'd be
"Would you like some tea?"

But I left my voice stranded
Somewhere between the parking lot and the waiting room
Where Dad is sitting
With a book in his lap
Pretending
Wishing he could concentrate
As these minutes
Slump past

I don't answer
But Taryn doesn't seem to mind
She simply stands
Walks across the room
To a small oak table
Where two ceramic mugs
Wait to be filled

Taryn trades me the clipboard for a mug
The weight feels good in my palms
The heat of the tea

Peppermint
Loosens my throat
Not that I'm ready to talk

Taryn sits back down
"This feels odd, doesn't it?"
I shrug
Knowing
Guessing it would be rude to say
Yes

"Maybe I should tell you a little about who I am and what I
    do."
Sure
I say

Because as long as she is
I won't have to
Talk

FIFTY MINUTES

We make a T-chart
Taryn and I
Like we do in school
Only this one is
Different

On the left is a list
Of the things my eating disorder gives me
On the right is a list
Of the things it has taken
From me

The words that fill the left side
Are easy to come up with
Pride
       Control
Power
       Strength
Thin, thinner, thin
Never thin
Enough

I only come up with one word
For the other side

Lonely

Maybe it is
Enough

AWKWARD SILENCE

Dad and I hide
Behind the music
Filling the truck
Neither of us sing along
Like we usually do
When the radio plays
Our favorite
Song

We're out of the city
Halfway home
Before he finally asks
"How was it?"
Fine, I say.
Because it was

"Are we going back again?"
Because it was my choice
He said it would be
As long as I gave it a try
Just once
That's all he'd asked

His knuckles are white
Against the black
Of the steering wheel
I know there is a right answer
To this question

I can't let my dad—my dog—my friends
Down again
Can't make it up to them
Everything that I've done
Wrong
But at least I can do this
For my dad

I guess.
"Because you don't—"
No. I want to.

I wrap my arm around Blue
Give his chest a scratch
That melts him across my lap
Tickle him under his arm
Set his hind leg kicking
Against Dad's hip
Knocking a smile loose
Onto his lips
Like only a dog's paw
Can do

IF YOU ARE, AM I?

"What do you think…"
I'm not sure which picture
Asia's talking about
When she lobs the question
Across the room
Into my lap

I look up
Checking to see what page she is on
Because we're sitting cross-legged on her bedroom floor
Looking at our new yearbooks

Which picture are you looking at?
"I'm not," she says
Letting her yearbook fall closed in her lap
"I mean, what do you think when you look at me?"

I'm confused
Because she looks perfect
Like she always does
Even when she's not trying
Leaning against her bed in a soft pink shirt
Jeans with holes in the knees
Her hair pulled back in a sloppy ponytail
Looking twice as good as I ever could
Even if I tried

"I'm just asking, because you think you're fat, right?"
No, I—

"Sure you do, otherwise you wouldn't have lost all that
   weight."
My thoughts tangle with the words in my throat
Making a knot
Heavy and hard
"I mean, do you feel disgusted when you look at me?"

In this moment
I get what's on the other side of this question
It's the way her eyes fall to her hands
Her knees come up to her chest
Turning her into a little girl
One who looks at herself in the mirror
Wanting to see more
Less
Someone
Something
Different
Than what she sees

Asia, you're perfect.
"That's what my mom always says."
A paper smile
Pale and thin
But you are. I'm not just saying that because you're my best friend.
"Good answer."
Asia reaches behind her
Grabs a pillow from her bed
Hurls it into my chest
Vulnerable girl gone

"Keep going," she says.

You're like a princess, I say.
"Like?"
You are *a princess*, I say.
Starting to laugh
Asia grabs a second pillow from her bed and cocks her arm
"Keep going."
Perfect in every way.
Asia puts the pillow down and sighs
"You've always been so tiny. I must seem—"
Like the best friend I could have ever asked for.
I mean it when I say it

Asia opens her yearbook again
Engrossed in the pictures
Of a team
Not even caring which one
And in the silence I know
My answer wasn't right

I wish I could explain
What it was
Is like
Fingers counting the bones
That were becoming
Me
That I could feel
But couldn't see
Because my body was
Is pieces
Jigsaw pieces that won't
Can't
Ever fit together

Because one was too big
Another just odd

I never judge anyone else because
There is no comparison
Everyone was
Is smaller than me
Fiction or fact
It didn't
Doesn't matter
Because all I see
Is me

Asia closes the yearbook and tosses it onto the bed
"You can talk to me, you know. I just want to understand."
So do I
I think
Peering across the hole that's between us
"Just try."

And I do
With splintered sentences
I begin to build a bridge
That isn't strong
Not now
But trusting
Knowing
That this is the only way
I'll be able to make this wrong
Into something
Close
To right

I owe it to Asia
And maybe I owe it
To me

CODY SAYS

"You're so lucky,
    being able to eat
    whatever you want."

I stare at the Tupperware container of trail mix
On the lunch table
In front of me
Ignoring the bag with the sandwich (a whole not a half) and
    fruit

Because really
He hates it
When girls
Don't
Eat

I'm listening
But not really
Because there are chocolate chips in the trail mix
Which just won't work
I pluck them out
One by one
Lining them up
Single file
On the Tupperware lid

Asia stopped listening
When the chocolate chips got in line
Reaches right through the middle of Cody's monologue

And calls them out
Those chocolate chips
So quiet and serene
She scoops them up
Pours them back
Into the trail mix

Cody leans across the table
Grabs a handful
Heavy on the chocolate I was trying to avoid
Tosses it into his mouth
Ignoring the death ray Asia shoots at him
With her eyes

Getting so thin
Isn't attractive
Nobody
Likes to hug
A skeleton
He says as he chews

Cody says
He never wanted to say this
Not when I was
Sick

Was sick
Means
Is well
I'm not sure
If that's

Right
The well part

Not yet
Anyway

CULPABLE

It's not
My fault
According to Dad
Dr. Larsen
Asia

But I sit on my lies
The ones I told
That no one saw
Not even
Especially not
Dad

And I know
Beyond a doubt
That it was
Is
My fault

When I asked Asia
How she knew
She showed me a book
About eating disorders
Not about me
Because that's what she'd learned
I didn't choose to have an eating disorder
I was
And am

More
Than this disease

Which makes me sad
In a way
Because if I'm not that
Then
What?

Which is sick
Sad
To miss this eating disorder
Like a friend
Though it is trying to kill me

This is the part I can never tell
Because it is
The worst lie
Of all
When I say I don't
Won't
Miss it at all
This disease that broke
So many people
I love

CHANGE

"We should do something
With your mom's room."
It was yours too.
I say
Because it was
Theirs
Not just hers
A lot like her
Life

Like what?
Dad shrugs
"I don't know. What would she—what would you—like?"
I look at the picture on the wall behind the kitchen table
Of the three of us
One of the only professional photos we ever had taken
Dad and I are smiling into the camera
But Mom
She's looking only at us
Happy

This picture makes me realize that they are one and the same
Whatever it is we—Dad and I—would like
Is what she would have wanted

It feels simpler
Easier
Thinking about it
That way

But the question still seems big
Heavy
Somehow

Dad pulls out the blender
Tosses in ice cream and berries
A splash of milk
Whhhhirrrrrr

This is the deal
He makes it
I eat it
No questions
Asked
This doesn't make me mad
Not like it used to
It feels easier
Not making the rules myself

"For you, my dear."
Dad sets the milkshake down
One for me
The other for him
He slides into the chair across from me
"We don't have to decide now. I just thought it was time."

I think about their room
About my mom
The way it felt when she hugged me
Before her arms became so thin
Her eyes grew too big
For her face

Thinking about this
Around this
I stare into my mug
And the numbers begin to stack
I can feel them in my chest
Heavy and slick
A domino tips

>A cup of milk—another of berries—120 plus 60—which
doesn't even include the ice cream—which makes another
250—which is fine—this is fine—until my stomach begins
to hurt from being so full though I haven't even taken a
drink—not a drink but a bite—I need a spoon because I
hate the feel of the ice cream on my top lip

So I walk
To the silverware drawer
"Will you grab me one too?" Dad asks.
Not noticing
The way the thoughts
Railroading through my mind have
Left my hands shaking
Sure.

It's not a problem
Eating this shake
I remind myself of this as I hand
Dad his spoon
And sit
Back down

"There's no rush. Something to think about," Dad repeats.

But it makes me nervous
This change
Dad has proposed
Now that it's out there
It seems like we should do something
Now
And whatever that is
It has to be
Right

I'm not sure what we should do.
My voice is in a hurry
With the room, I mean.
"We can try out a few ideas and, if they don't work, we can try
    something else."

Dad dips his spoon into his shake
Takes a bite
He doesn't even think about it
The calories
        fat
                    grams of sugar
                        carbs
I wonder if
When
I'll be able to do that
Maybe someday
One day
Just not today

I stab at a glob of ice cream
Floating in my shake
Maybe that's the secret
Knowing the answer
Doesn't have to be perfect
Even when it comes

RUDE AWAKENING

My sheets choked me awake
Tangled around my torso
Knotted at my knees
Blankets at my feet
Pajamas soaked
Wet through
With sweat
Last night

I thought it was the dream
The bad dream
I'd had
The one where I slid through a pond
Shallow enough to fill my eyes
Deep enough to cover my toes
So deep
I couldn't breathe

It happened again
An hour later
There was no dream this time
Just the waking up
The sweating
Through the clean pajamas I put on
After I woke
Up
The first time

I'm thinking about those wet pajamas
Balled at the bottom of my hamper
As I stand in the middle of the school library
I didn't know who to ask about
Something so embarrassing
So I thought I'd look
Here

The computers are full
My goal was to slip into one of the orange plastic chairs
In front of an anonymous screen
That wouldn't giggle
Couldn't joke
About my situation
Knowledge base
Zero

But now that I'm standing
Between these shelves of books
That smell like dust
I don't know where to look
A journal
A book

"Good morning, Raesha!"
I spin around
Caught
In the middle of what?
Miss Pattinson pushes a cart of books up the aisle
Good morning.
"Don't tell me. Let me guess. AP History. Final paper."

I can feel my cheeks flush pink
If only
Yes. I haven't even started.
"You and everyone else it seems."
Miss Pattinson pushes her cat-eye glasses off her nose
As she tips her head toward the entrance
"There's a whole cart of books I pulled for your class by the
circulation desk."

Thank you.
The warning bell bleats
Five minutes until class
Which is fine
I'll go
To class
It's not like I needed to know

I'll just forget about it
Until tonight
Maybe it won't happen
Again

FOLLOW-UP EXAM

It's a funny thing to remember
That day
The choice
That, at the time, didn't mean
Anything

I stepped off a cliff and onto the scale
Exactly six months ago today
Never knowing
Never dreaming
That I would ever end up
Here

Because I'm not
One of those girls
Who says she's fat
So she can hear someone tell her
She's not

I wasn't then
Am not now
Even though I know I'm not
Thin

Not anymore
I hold that thought in my head
I'm not
Thin

As we walk through the door and into Dr. Larsen's office
Thirty days out
My first weigh-in

BACKWARD

They're called blind weighs
I didn't know that last time I was here
Kami just asked me to step on the scale
Backward
So I did
Not really minding
What with my own scale back at home

But I mind now
Am still mad
Sitting on the exam table in my paper gown
Because that's what I had to wear to be weighed
No street clothes
No shoes
Just this

Dr. Larsen comes in
Clipboard in hand
"Raesha, how are you?"
Fine.
My voice is gravel
Sharp in my throat
"How are you feeling?"
Fine.
"How are you doing with your meal plan?"
Fine.

Dr. Larsen raises her eyebrows
"You don't sound fine."

I shrug

Hating myself for acting so truculent to this woman who has
    never been anything but kind

I glance at the photograph of the border collie on her wall

The dog's name is Daisy

I met her when she was a pup

Dr. Larsen had brought her to the hospital one night when I
    was there with Dad

Waiting for Mom

Daisy couldn't come in

But I went out

To Dr. Larsen's truck and held Daisy's fuzzy puppy body

Wriggling and licking

Dr. Larsen had said she just happened to be there

Had to work at the hospital that night

Somehow I don't think she had to work that night

At all

I sigh

Almost manage a smile

I'm sorry. I'm tired, I guess.

"I bet. How are you sleeping? Any night sweats?"

Night sweats?

"It happens when your metabolism gets going again.
    Essentially, you're burning so many calories that your body
    gets hot and you sweat during the night. Has this happened
    at all?"

A bit.

"Your metabolism is going through the roof.

But that's what happens when the refeeding process begins,"
  Dr. Larsen says.

It's hard to keep the anger in check
Because why didn't someone mention this before?
What else don't I know?

"How much weight do you think you've gained?"
A lot. At least ten pounds.
"Two."
I look for the crack in the conversation
That swallowed the joke
       Only two pounds?
       Impossible
Already deciding that this is it
I'm not coming back
No more appointments
No matter what Dad says
"Two pounds. You've gained exactly two pounds."
That can't be right. I've been eating so much.

"You've been healing from the inside out. It's like I told you,
  the weight doesn't come back all at once. Your metabolism
  has gone from zero to sixty in less than thirty days."
I'm nodding and she's talking
My exchanges are going up
My meals will be even bigger
Which is fine
I guess

But it still doesn't make sense
Not that any part of this disease ever did

But the getting well
That should be logical
Predictable
Doctor's orders after all

But now
Even this
Gaining weight
A timeline for getting well
It can't be
Predicted

Can't be
Controlled

EXPECTATIONS SHATTERED

Dad is talking to Kami when I come out of the exam room
"I make sure she is eating everything on her meal plan," he
    says. "I prepare it myself."
"I know you do," Kami replies. "Her vitals look great. It just
    takes time."
"But she isn't gaining the weight back."
"It's slow going at first," Kami says. "It takes time."

I slip off to the side
Melting into one of the chairs in the corner of the waiting room
As Dr. Larsen approaches Dad
We can do more
Will work harder
Dad tells her

"I can't lose her, Dr. Larsen," Dad says. "Not her too."
That's when I see tears fall
From my dad's eyes
First one
Then more
Running down his cheeks

The fissures erupt
My heart breaks in half
Because he hasn't cried like this
Not in front of me
Not even after Mom

"It's not your fault."
Dr. Larsen says.
"You're going to make it through this, just wait and see."

I should tell him
She's right
It was never his fault
Not Mom
Not this
None of it was him

But I don't
Because my words don't matter
Not after so many lies
In all the months leading up to now
I'll have to show him
That she's right

We are going to make it through this
Dad and I

WHEN THEY ASK

"You could
Put your arm in a sling
Tell everyone Micah's little sister
Beat you up,"
Asia suggests
And laughs

"Or Fancy—
Tell people she's lame
Navicular
Thrush
No!
A bone spur!"

Until we show up next fall and everyone sees she's sound.
I turn away
Distracted
By the bargain basket of dog toys
At the end of the aisle

Blue hasn't ever loved stuffed animals
Finds chasing a ball demeaning
But still
I like to look
I always go home with something
From the feed store
For him

Asia shrugs
"It's none of their business why you're not riding. It's just—"
She stops to run her fingers over a headstall
With hand-tooled silver
Hanging from the endcap
Before turning down the aisle
Lined with leashes and food bowls
For animals too small
To live
In the barn

"It will be so strange without you there. You've never missed a
    single rodeo. Ever."
I know. I just...

I wish I could explain
What it felt like
To see Dad
In the doctor's office yesterday

If it weren't for those tears
I'd probably lie to him
Would definitely ride
At the rodeo this weekend
The last one
Before State
But I can't do that
To him
Can't break another thing
That I love

"Is it selfish that I want you there?" Asia asks.
No. I'd be mad if you didn't.
Which is true
But sadly
So is this
*I just don't want to answer any questions. It's embarrassing enough
    as it is.*
"It's not like anyone knows."
Which isn't true

The story of a girl like me
With a disease like this
Burned up and down the halls at school
Spread to the other teams
Where my competitors
Pretended to be sad
Not-so-secretly glad
That Fancy and I stepped out
Leaving a spot to Nationals
Wide open

Asia shoves her hands into her pockets
Searching for the list Alexi gave us
Before we walked out the door
The list I plucked
From the seat of the truck
Where it slid
During our drive
Into town
"I can't believe we're shopping for a rabbit."

Technically, seven rabbits.
I take a plastic hedgehog from the basket
Knowing Blue will love the squeaker inside
Drop it into Asia's shopping basket as I hand her
The list

She unfolds the paper
And groans
"Who is this kid? Seriously! Look at this!"
Each line item numbered
Words spelled out carefully
In glittery green

#1 BPA-free plastic water bottle
#2 rabbit hammock—organic cotton—not pink!

I look at Asia
Standing in front of the rabbit accoutrements
Lining the shelves
And try not to smile
Can rabbits even see in color?
"Who cares? They're rabbits!"

Asia grabs a water bottle
Turns it in her hands
Looking for the label
"How am I supposed to know if this thing is BPA-free?"
I guess if Alexi's rabbit gets cancer, we know whose fault it was.

My joke trips
On reality
Falling flat on the floor

The C-word
Can do that

Asia steps around the joke
And puts the water bottle in her basket
"If anyone asks—"
Which they will.
"Just tell them you've been sick. Leave it at that."

Asia pulls a rabbit hammock from the shelf
Green with stripes
Drops it into her basket
"But remind them they'd better watch out for you next year."

Next year
I think
That's what I tell myself

Maybe
    Definitely
Next
    Year

AMBIVALENCE

This is what I miss
Being in control
Of my body

Feeling thin and light
With a secret
All my own
So good at this trick
Called thinner
       thinner
          gone

This is the part I don't miss
That I have to remind myself about
When I want
To go back

The way my moods flew
From one side of the sky
To the other
Black clouds
Lightning cracked
Fall into the deepest blue

Always cold
Fingers numb
My heart a hummingbird in my chest
And tired

Always
So, so tired

Scared of the leavings
That would come
With the knowing
If Cody
     Asia
My dad
Please don't (do)
Find out
I'd prayed

The goal that I had
That could never be reached
Or did I hate (love)
This part?
The most

The way I felt when I messed up
Fucked up
Let the food in
Had to force it out
Before it was calories and fat

Because it wasn't worth it
All that sacrifice
To be thin
At least that's what I tell
Myself

AFTER HOURS

It's an off night
Tuesday night
No team practice
Just the three of us
In the arena
Two on horses
Me in the stands
Cupping the video camera
To my eye

First for Asia
Now Kierra
Sitting tall in her saddle
On her buckskin gelding
Under the flannel gray
Sky

Motionless
As she runs through the reining pattern
In her head
The part of the queen contest
That will come after the interview
Before the fashion show
At State
Next week

Kierra nods in my direction
My cue
To let the camera roll

I lean forward
Press the record button
As Kierra picks up the inside rein
Lays down the outside
Spins to the left
Three
Two
One
Then the right

Picks up her inside lead
For the clockwise circles
Large and fast
Small and slow

I zoom in
Catch the flying lead change
Counterclockwise now
Large and fast
Small and slow

The hoofprint shadows
They leave in the dirt
Show Asia and I
What Kierra will see
When she watches the video
Concentric circles
Collected precision
The kind that's almost impossible
To beat

Kierra flattens herself
Along her horse's neck
Throws her reins away
Kicks her gelding
Into a gallop

Up the rail
Sit down hard
A sliding stop
Insert score
Hand Kierra
The crown

That's how it's going to go
On Saturday
If she rides half as good
As she did
Just now

Asia lets out a whoop
From the far end of the arena
Where she and Scuba are waiting
Kierra looks in my direction
For the wave I give
To let her know I got it
All on film

I know Asia isn't going to do another run
Not after that
Picture-perfect pattern

I tuck my camera into the case
Dangling from my shoulder
Begin walking down the stairs
Toward Asia's truck
Away from the arena

As the two of them ride
Side by side
Around the arena
Cooling their horses down

Just like they will
On Saturday
When I won't
Be there

FRIDAY NIGHT

Micah and Asia
Cody and me
Step out of the movie theater
Onto the sidewalk
Half-empty drink cups
Still in our hands
Laughing over the movie that hadn't been bad
Could have been better

They're excited
I pretend to be
About the tomorrow they'll have
That I won't
"Set your alarm!" Cody says to Micah
Who laughs
Because how could he not
Remember to set his clock
For the last qualifying rodeo of the year?

Asia lets go of Micah's hand
Pulls me into a hug
"Think about coming?" she says into my ear.
She smiles when she pulls back
But her eyes are sad
Because we both know
I won't

If I'm there
In the stands

Without a horse
Of my own
People
Will talk

  Too sick to ride. Didn't you hear?
As if I don't
Know
What it is
They're saying

Asia grabs Micah's hand again
Throws a good-bye over her shoulder
As they dash across the street
To where Micah's truck
Is parked

Cody wraps his arm
Around my waist
Kisses my neck
As we make our way down the sidewalk
To where his truck
Is parked
He opens my door
Closes it after me

I climb in
Flip the sun visor down
Squinting into the mirror
Searching for a lash
In my eye
That isn't there
Pretending this is the reason

For the tears
I catch on my fingertip
Before he climbs in

I wish
I want
But I won't let myself
Cry
Because probably
Maybe
I'll have another chance
At Nationals
Next year

SECOND HALF OF THE NIGHT

It doesn't take long
To get out of Salida Springs
Off the main street
Into the night

Cody pulls the truck off the road
Into the grass that's part of the park at the edge of town
He knows I love to hear the creek that runs down its middle
Folks have started pulling water off it for irrigating
Draining the creek thin and quiet
Cody knows I still like it here
Even when I can't hear
What I know is there

Cody puts the truck in park
Changes the music
To something new
Something slow
I take my seat belt off
Lean into him
As he sits back
In his seat

"I wish you were coming," he says.
Knees to my chest
I look away
Eyes searching for stars
In the night sky

Thinking about the fact that the stars aren't even there
Not anymore

Ignoring the tears
Running down my cheeks
While Cody
Just holds me
Lets me
Cry

EMPTY SADDLE

Dad and I
Are making dinner
Lasagna
With noodles of eggplant
When the phone rings

I'm glad
For the distraction
From this meal
That smells
So good
It actually makes my stomach
Growl
Which makes me hate
Myself
For being
So weak

"Can you get that," Dad asks
As he opens the oven door
To sprinkle a little more cheese
On another meal
I don't
Want to eat

I nod
Grab the phone
Head into the living room
Before answering

Because I know
Who it is

"I'm going to Nationals! Barrels and pole bending!"
Asia yells
Before I can even say hi
I knew you would!
Trying to match her excitement
With my voice
What about the queen contest?
"Kierra won. I'm so happy for her!"

It's hard to hear Asia
Over the music
Crackling through the speakers
Above riders
Yelling congratulations to each other
The announcer
Calling out the final standings
"I miss you, Rae! I seriously can't believe you aren't here!"

If I were, I'd be giving you a huge hug.
I can hear Cody now
Can picture him riding up behind Asia
As he calls
"Is that Rae? Let me talk to her!"

"Wait!" Asia says
But the telephonic thunk
Of fingers to phone
Tells me
That Cody swiped her phone

"Hey, I miss you, babe."
Miss you too. How'd you do?
"Silver State."
I sit down on the couch
Tucking my feet under me
I knew you would.

"Just hold on!"
Cody shouts at Micah
Who wants the key to the tack room
That he has in his back pocket

"Guess I better go. I'll call you tonight," Cody says.
Congratulations.
I say again
Not knowing if he hears me
Before hanging up
Quicker than I thought
He would

"How'd everyone do?"
Dad asks
As he comes into the living room
Good.

Fishing the remote from between the cushions
Looking for that show
Some show
Any show
That I can't wait to watch
Too absorbed in what's happening on the screen to talk to Dad
About the results of the day

That should have been
Mine

Dad sits down next to me
Takes the remote
Turns up the volume
On this program
Neither of us
Care anything about

Dad puts his arm
Around my shoulders
Pulls me to him
Never taking his eyes from the television
Knowing eye contact
Now
Would simply be
Too much

"This isn't forever," Dad says. "There's always next year."
I know he's right
But sometimes I wonder
How I'm going to make it
To next year
When today
Feels like more
Than I can
Handle

TABITHA TWITCHET'S TEA PARTY

It seems like everything revolves around food
I really don't think it's me
Being eating-disordered
Because today is another
Day
That revolves around
Food
Or it will be
If I let it

Lacey runs over to the round table in the library
I have claimed
For her and me
She has two paper plates
There's a sugar cookie on each one
"Isn't this the best?" Lacey asks.
As she climbs into the chair next to mine

"Did you know I get to take a book home for my own? We
    pick them at the end. A cookie and a book."
She says this last part almost to herself
In wonder
But this is an amazing event
Tabitha Twitchet's Annual Tea Party
A special occasion just for us
The reading buddy pairs

"Here you are, my dears." Mr. Monroe says.
Grade-school librarian and party host extraordinaire

Sets two cups of chamomile tea in front of us

"Thank you," Lacey says, peering into her cup.

She waits until he walks away to ask

"What is this?"

Tea. Like in the book.

Lacey looks at me blankly

The Tale of Tom Kitten?

She shrugs

"He'll read it to us soon."

Lacey takes a bite of her cookie and nods

I glance around the room

Ignoring the cookie on my plate

The other reading buddies

Are getting situated

Sitting in twos and fours

With their cookies and their cups of chamomile tea

I didn't know there were so many reading partners

First-, second-, third-graders all in pairs

With people like me

A few of the reading buddies are in high school

But most are not

They're older

Grandparent-aged volunteers

I feel as if they're all looking at me

Like they all know

About the lies I've told

The weight I've lost

They're watching me

Waiting to see

If I
Eat

It's silly
But in a town as small as this
How could they not
Know?

"You're still going to come though, aren't you? Even after the
    party?" Lacey asks.
Her voice pulls me back to reality
Sure. Why wouldn't I?
Lacey glances around the room
Drops her voice to a whisper
"Some people get a new buddy every year. I was hoping I could
    keep you."

Keep me
That's what she said
This little girl with sun-streaked braids
Sitting beside me in turtle-patched jeans
Able to say what she thinks
Ask for what she wants

"Who's ready for a story?" Mr. Monroe asks,
Striding to the front of the group
"As you know, Beatrix Potter's books tend to be a bit on the
    small side."
He holds up a pint-sized edition of *The Tale of Tom Kitten*
"So I'm going to put the pictures on the screen for you to see
    while I read."
Mr. Monroe flips off the lights and starts the projector

Lacey reaches over
Grabs my arm
Gives it a pull
Wanting me to move closer
To her
So I do

Without taking her eyes off the screen
And the picture of a little brown kitten
In a blue shirt and pants
She picks up my cookie
Hands it to me
As she nibbles her own

It's easier somehow
In the dark
That smells like chamomile
To take a bite
First one
Then two
Knowing that someone
My Lacey, our Lacey
Is glad
She gets to keep
Me

BLANK PAGES

I bought this book
And in it
I write
About the things I can't talk about
Not even to Blue

Someday I'll share
Just not
Now

PAPER PACKAGES

Books arrive in the mail
Addressed to my dad
Read by him
Passed on
To me

Books about me
For me
So we can better
Understand
This disease

I like them
These books
With the real-life stories
About girls like me
Who have forgotten
How to
Eat

Sometimes these girls
Get better
But other times
They don't

I wish I could have it
Both ways
Getting well
Staying thin

But I know
I'm going to have
To make
A choice

REPUTABLE SOURCES

They say it is
   Genetics
      Perfectionism
   Depression
    Anxiety
      Media
   Trauma
A combination
  of factors
    really

They say it is
      An addiction
A disease that devours
    Bodies in its path

They say it is
   Falling down
      Standing up
   Trip and fall
    Again

They say it is
The nature
  of this
Disease
    Relapse (inevitable)

They say it is
      Worth it
All this work
   I'm doing

I hope they are right
About this last part
Anyway

ROUNDUP

We started this morning
Before the sun leaked across the sky
When the steers were stiff and slow with cold

It was like it has always been
Men and women and kids
Slumped up against pickup trucks
Inhaling the steam off their coffee
All in chinks and boots with jingling spurs

Horses tacked up
Lead ropes looped through the slats of the stock trailers
And the dogs zipping in and out of it all
Heeler dogs
Cow-eating machines

And me and Asia
Best friends since forever
First to mount up and be ready to go
Not caring that the calves set for sorting
Won't wear our brands
We'll work hard
All the same
To give this family a start
A dad and his girls
Not so new to these parts

Riding into it now
Swinging their ropes 'round

Turning two into three
Kierra and her muscle-thick quarter horse
Working in with Asia and me
As we peel them off
One calf
Sometimes two

Alexi and Lacey
Cheering from the green panel fence
As the ropes start flying

First bull calf of the day
Kierra's dad and mine
Catch him up
Lay him down
Stretched out lean
Bawling at the smoke rolling off his iron-branded hide

More folks riding into it now
Neighbors-parents-brothers-sisters-aunts-uncles-cousins
It's all the same today
When even a family that's just three
Suddenly has more family than they can count
Spread out all around them
Beneath a sky
Breathed blue

HAPPY ENDING

I wish I could tell you
That I'm fine
Better now
That things are back
To the way
They were

But it can't be
The same
Can't go back
To the way it was

Whatever
It
Whoever
I
Was

Because I'm different now
Not better
Not worse
Just
    different

STATISTICS

In the United States, as many as ten million women and one million men are struggling with an eating disorder. Eating disorders have the highest mortality rate of any mental health condition. The mortality rate associated with anorexia nervosa is twelve times higher than the death rate of all causes of death for females between fifteen and twenty-four years of age.

Unfortunately, treatment for eating disorders is costly, and in many cases, impossible for individuals and their families to access. Only one out of ten people with eating disorders will receive treatment. Of these, only forty percent fully recover.

For more information about eating disorders and their treatment, please visit the National Eating Disorders Association's website: www.nationaleatingdisorders.org.

AUTHOR'S NOTE

This book is the truest, most important thing I will ever write. I remember thinking I was fat when I was five, wishing my hips and thighs were gone at seven, and feeling powerful when I pushed away from the table in the school cafeteria at twelve. As a teen and later as an adult, I lost jobs. I lost friends. I lost myself.

When I finally realized I needed help, I attempted to admit myself to a treatment facility, but there were problems. I had no insurance, little money, and even less in the way of personal support. After being turned away from one treatment center after another, a door finally opened.

I went to treatment not once, not twice, but three times, emerging stronger and more committed to recovery each time. Today, and every day, I make a choice to eat. I make a choice to participate in life and to take risks. I am a mother, a teacher, and a writer. I am so much more than a disease.

If you are in the throes of an eating disorder, I'd like to say this to you: Don't give up. Life is glorious, tragic, unpredictable, exciting, and mundane. Life is all those things. Give yourself permission to experience them. You are worth it.

ACKNOWLEDGMENTS

First and foremost, I would like to thank my agent, Sara Scuito. We started with a poem and ended with a book. Your faith in this novel never wavered. Thank you for your patience, gentle prodding, and invaluable insight. I'd also like to thank Annette Pollert-Morgan and the rest of the crew at Sourcebooks. I could not have asked for a truer team to champion Raesha's story.

It was at Vermont College of Fine Arts that this book first emerged and where I truly learned what it takes to be a writer. Thank you to Alison McGhee and Ron Koertge for your critical eye and encouraging words. Susan Fletcher, had you not suggested I attend the Willamette Writer's Conference in Portland, I might not have ever found an agent and this book a home. Kathi Appelt, you are an inspiration as not only an author but a teacher. Norma Fox Mazer, you were one of the greats. I owe so much of who I am as a writer to you. Thank you.

A most gracious thank you to Dr. Katy Byrd for not only answering questions about everything from pulling calves to treating colicing horses, but for your friendship through the years. Rachel Hawes, you picked up where Katy left off, answering my every question about high school rodeo. I wish Al Peterson were still here to see this book because he contributed more than he will ever know. His stories about ropings, rodeos, and everything in between helped me capture the energy of some of the most pivotal scenes in this book. Melissa Chandler, even when you were balancing your own writing and caring for your brand-new baby girl, you still made time to read and respond to the ridiculously voluminous rough drafts I sent. I raise my Dunkin' Donuts coffee in thanks to you.

In so many ways, the journey of writing this book mirrored that of my own recovery from an eating disorder. The clinicians at St. Vincent's Eating Disorder Program had a list of reasons why they could have, and honestly probably should have, turned me away. They didn't, however and, in the words of the staff there, you showed me how to save my own life. Dr. Marianne Weaver, you picked up where my treatment team at St. Vincent's left off. Thank you for continuing to guide me on my journey.

And to my daughter, Lillian Alene, you have shown me joy like I have never known. I love you deeply and recklessly, now and forever.

ABOUT THE AUTHOR

Catherine Alene has an MA in teaching, and she earned her MFA in writing at Vermont College of Fine Arts. Like the protagonist in *The Sky Between You and Me*, Catherine battled anorexia nervosa. Now in recovery, she is actively involved with the National Eating Disorders Association (NEDA) and regularly serves as a recovery speaker, talking to college students and professional groups about her experience living with, and finally recovering from, the disease. Catherine teaches language arts at an alternative high school in central Oregon, where she currently lives with her daughter, horse, cat, and black lab, Herman.